W9-AFK-714

THE WILD WORLD *of* BUCK BRAY
THE WOLVES *of* SLOUGH CREEK

BOOK THREE

WHAT READERS ARE SAYING ABOUT
THE WILD WORLD
OF BUCK BRAY BOOKS

"Something for everyone—adventure, suspense, geography, and science! Buck Bray's exciting adventure is a story that keeps readers in suspense. This mystery is one you won't want to put down. I can't wait to read more of Buck's wild adventures through our amazing country."
—**Royce Wilkinson, Wellsville-Middleton Elementary, Wellsville, Missouri**

"*Danger at the Dinosaur Stomping Grounds* is an outstanding story. There is a good balance of mystery, unexpected surprises, and humor. As the story goes on, it continues to get more mysterious and more exciting. I enjoyed the book!"
—**Barret Malouf, Winterberry Charter School, Anchorage, Alaska**

"The Wild World of Buck Bray books are not your usual mystery stories. They are amazing adventures that include solving mysteries, overcoming problems, and facing life-threatening situations!"
—**Jordan Cassetto, Heights Elementary, Clarkston, Washington**

"*The Missing Grizzly Cubs* is a very suspenseful book that you can't put down. It keeps you in mystery until the very end!"
—**Dylan Wortham, Hopewell Middle School, Round Rock, Texas**

"I like the adventure and the cool locations, the way the stories take place in national parks. And I like how they add the videography to the mysteries. Buck is an interesting character, and I want to read more of his adventures."
—**Forrest Athearn, Denver School of Science and Technology/Byers, Denver, Colorado**

"Buck Bray is a modern boy with lots of technology at his fingertips, but he combines common sense, help from his friends, and lots of adventure to solve mysteries at some of America's most popular national parks. I'm anxiously awaiting Buck's next adventure so I can travel along and visit another national park through his eyes . . . and try to solve the mystery along with him!"
—**Susan Hutchins, Semi-Retired Literacy/Special Education Teacher, Poudre School District, Fort Collins, Colorado**

"What child doesn't love camping, dinosaurs, and a mystery to solve? As part of a literacy parent engagement activity, Portland Elementary purchased an autographed copy of *Danger of the Dinosaur Stomping Grounds* for each of our families. We gave our families weekly reading assignments and had Judy visit our school to do writing workshops with each of our classes."
—**Cristy West, Portland Elementary Principal, Portland, Arkansas**

"I just finished *The Missing Grizzly Cubs* and loved it! This book would be great for students who love adventure stories. I also enjoyed the bear facts that titled each chapter and the education about being a good steward of our national parks. I've ordered the next Wild World of Buck Bray and can't wait for it to arrive."
—**Ginger Addicott, Third-Grade Teacher, Chain Lake Elementary, Monroe, Washington**

Text copyright © 2019 Judy Young
Cover illustration copyright © 2019 Celia Krampien
Design copyright © 2019 Sleeping Bear Press

Sleeping Bear Press™

2395 South Huron Parkway, Suite 200, Ann Arbor, MI 48104
www.sleepingbearpress.com
© Sleeping Bear Press

Printed and bound in the United States.
10 9 8 7 6 5 4 3 2 1

Library of Congress Cataloging-in-Publication Data
Names: Young, Judy, 1956- author.
Title: The wolves of Slough Creek / written by Judy Young.
Description: Ann Arbor, MI : Sleeping Bear Press, [2019] | Series: The Wild World of Buck Bray ; book 3 | Summary: Eleven-year-olds Buck and Toni and the Wild World of Buck Bray television crew head to Yellowstone National Park to film an episode about its famous geysers and gray wolf restoration program, but soon after arriving they suspect someone is operating drones illegally in the park.
Identifiers: LCCN 2018037164|
ISBN 9781534110205 (hardcover) | ISBN 9781534110212 (pbk.)
Subjects: LCSH: Yellowstone National Park--Juvenile fiction. | CYAC: Yellowstone National Park--Fiction. | Television programs--Production and direction--Fiction. | Wolves--Fiction. | Drone aircraft--Fiction. | Mystery and detective stories.
Classification: LCC PZ7.Y8664 Wo 2019 | DDC [Fic]--dc23
LC record available at https://lccn.loc.gov/2018037164

For Tucker,
who will have many of his own
wild world adventures!

–Love, Grandma

With special thanks to:

Philo West, campground host extraordinaire,
for many enjoyable and entertaining chats around campfires
at Box Canyon, Idaho.

Mike Baer, Principal,
for the tour of Gardiner School.
Go Bruins!

and

The rangers, park employees, and wolf spotters
I consulted concerning this book,
for all they do keeping Yellowstone National Park
"for the benefit and enjoyment of the people."

J.Y.

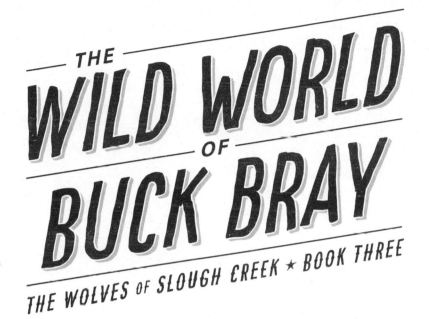

THE WILD WORLD OF BUCK BRAY

OF

THE WOLVES OF SLOUGH CREEK ★ BOOK THREE

JUDY YOUNG

PUBLISHED BY SLEEPING BEAR PRESS

When we try to pick out anything by itself,
we find it hitched to everything else in the Universe.

—John Muir

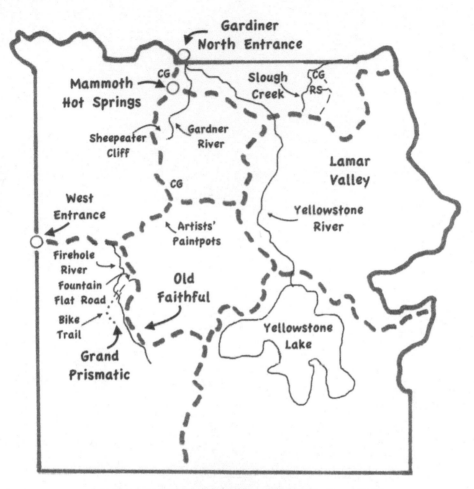

YELLOWSTONE NATIONAL PARK

TAKE 1:

"IF A BISON RACED A WOLF, THEY'D TIE! BOTH CAN REACH 35 MILES PER HOUR."

THURSDAY, MAY 15

Buck was so distracted as he walked across the parking lot that he didn't notice the thunderous roar coming up from behind him until Toni screamed. Buck quickly spun around. Charging straight toward him was a wall of bison. Dust filled the air as they stampeded through the piney woods beside Yellowstone's Firehole River. Branches snapped as the huge beasts plowed over small trees and trampled deadfalls in their path. Before Buck could even think, the herd stormed into the parking lot, the noise of their stomping hooves becoming even more deafening when they hit the pavement.

In the lead was the biggest bull bison of the herd. Its small, beady eyes set wide apart in its enormous head seemed to focus on Buck. As it entered the parking lot, it lowered its head, exposing the huge hump of its back, its horns now curved forward. It let out a snort that steamed from its nostrils in the chilly air. Then it veered toward Buck, the rest of the herd following. Buck turned and ran for the closest thing he saw—a white SUV with a dark green stripe. But the sound of hooves pounding from behind gained on him rapidly, and he knew he wasn't going to make it. He still had twenty yards to go before he could reach safety behind the SUV, when he was slammed to the ground.

As his breath was knocked from him, Buck instinctively closed his eyes and curled into a ball, waiting to be trampled to almost certain death. Then something grabbed hold of him and pulled him backward. Thinking one of the bison's horns had hooked his belt, Buck's muscles tensed even more, expecting to be tossed into the air. When he didn't go flying, Buck opened his eyes.

The fury of the beating hooves stomping on pavement continued as dozens of bison legs raced past him only inches away. But a woman in a green ranger uniform had hold of his belt. She had tugged him backward toward where she squatted, hunched behind a big boulder in the middle of the parking lot. Buck quickly scooted closer to her, and the woman put her arm around him, pulling him even tighter to her side. They both huddled up against the rock, their knees bent tight to their chests. They sat that way for only a minute or two, but to Buck it seemed like hours that the living wall of brown beasts stampeded around them.

———+—·

An hour before, eleven-year-old Buck and his father, along with their cameraman, Shoop, and Shoop's eleven-year-old daughter, Toni, had entered Yellowstone National Park through the west entrance before the sun was even up. They were headed to Old Faithful, where they were to meet a ranger who would help them as they filmed another episode of *The Wild World of Buck Bray* television series. Buck kept his eyes peeled, looking through the window that connected the living area with the cab of the camper. He hoped to see some wildlife, but in the headlights that split the darkness he saw nothing but road.

"Are we there?" Buck asked when Dad slowed the Green Beast down and turned right.

"No, it says here that it will be at least another forty minutes depending on traffic before we reach Old Faithful," Toni answered, using a flashlight to read from some information pamphlets they had gotten at the entrance.

Buck yawned and rubbed his eyes, trying to stay awake, but it wasn't long before his eyes shut and his head bobbed. As they continued, the sun started peeking over the mountains to their left, turning the sky pink, but Buck didn't notice. He was sound asleep, his cheek resting on the back of the couch by the window.

"Pull in there!" Shoop suddenly shouted.

Buck startled awake as Dad quickly swung the Green Beast onto a short drive leading to a parking lot.

"Look how the light is filtering through the steam coming off the Firehole!" Shoop continued.

"Firehole?" Buck asked, quickly looking out the window.

"That's the name of the river we've been driving alongside," Toni said.

In the early morning light the river shimmered in a sparkling flow of fluid silver. Plumes of steam rose from it. Steam also dotted its banks, looking like the smoke from dozens of campfires, twisting and turning with spiraling tendrils. The rising sun caught droplets of water in the steam, and, magically, bits of moving rainbows flickered as the vapor swirled and rose.

"That would make a great opening shot!" Shoop said.

"We've got plenty of time," Dad said, glancing at his watch. "We're not scheduled to meet the ranger until eight."

"Where are we?" Buck asked.

"Grand Prismatic Spring," Dad answered. "It's only a few more miles to Old Faithful."

"Listen to this," Toni said. She started reading aloud again. "Grand Prismatic Spring is the largest hot spring in the United States and is photographed more than anything else in Yellowstone."

"How big is it?" Buck asked.

"It says it's bigger than a football field," Toni replied.

Dad pulled into a parking space next to a black pickup. It had a shell covering the truck bed and a camping trailer hooked to the back. Without hesitating, Shoop grabbed the backpack that held his camera equipment. He jumped out of the cab before they had even come to a complete stop.

"Bring the shotgun mic and meet me at that footbridge, Toni," Shoop said, and started jogging across the parking lot.

Toni swung her red backpack over one shoulder and picked up a black case. Inside it was a microphone that attached to an extending pole, and a pair of headphones. Stepping from the camper, she hurried after her father. Buck followed her out the door. The early May air was cold. Buck stretched, then jammed his hands into the pocket of his gray hoodie. As he waited for his father to gather script notebooks and lock the camper, he watched Shoop and Toni cut across the long, rectangular parking lot to the wooden footbridge. Beyond it, clouds of steam billowed from the huge expanse of Grand Prismatic Spring.

A car backed out of a space near the footbridge and drove around several large boulders strategically placed at the far end of the lot to direct the flow of traffic back out to the main road. Beyond the boulders, Buck saw nothing but a forest of tall lodgepole pine.

"I wish they'd put the long parking spots for RVs and campers closer to the front for once," Buck whined as he watched Shoop and Toni step onto a sidewalk that led to the bridge.

"It won't hurt you to walk a bit," Dad said, "and it'll give you time to rehearse the script."

Buck rolled his eyes. He had read the scripts so many times, he felt as if he could say them in his sleep. As he and his father headed toward the bridge, Buck heard a vehicle drive in behind them, and soon some voices.

"That's the weirdest-looking camper I've ever seen," a girl's voice said.

Buck glanced back over his shoulder. An RV that had

SEE AMERICA FIRST written in huge letters across the side had pulled in next to their camper. A man, a woman, and two kids—a boy and a girl—had gotten out of it. They stood staring at the Brays' camper that looked like a combination of a tank and a school bus.

"'Bray Traveling Studio. The Wild World of Buck Bray,'" the woman said, reading aloud the wording on the camper's door. "I wonder what that's all about."

"Beats me," the girl said, then she turned to the boy. "Race you!"

The two kids took off running, quickly passing Buck and his father.

"Don't go any farther than the bridge," the man's voice called out. Soon, the woman and the man had caught up with Buck and his father. The man said hello, and Dad returned the greeting, but Buck didn't stick around for what he knew was going to happen next. He jogged on ahead, hearing the man ask Dad the usual question, "Are you making a movie or something?"

When Buck reached the bridge, Shoop had the tripod set up on the sidewalk nearby. The camera was mounted to it, and he was already filming the steam rising from the river and its banks. Toni and the two kids from the SEE AMERICA FIRST RV were standing in the middle of the bridge.

"That's Buck," Toni said as Buck approached them. "And this is Kale and Kayla Kolson. They're twins and the same age as us."

"Hi," Buck said. "I saw you get out of your RV."

"You've got a wicked-looking camper," Kayla said.

"Yeah, we call it the Green Beast," Buck said.

"Ours is just a rental," Kayla said. "It's the first time our family has ever gone camping."

"That's cool," Buck said. "It's a lot of fun."

"Toni told us about your show," Kayla continued. "Could we watch you being filmed?"

"Sure," Buck said, shrugging. Then, leaning his elbows on the bridge railing, he looked upstream. Without saying a word, Kale stood next to Buck, leaning his elbows on the bridge, too.

The two sides of the river were totally different from each other. Open lodgepole woods on the left side sloped gently to the river. Upstream, beyond the trees, a grassy meadow lined the river as it curved. On the right side of the river there were no trees or grassy meadows. The bank was made of solid stone rising steeply from the river's edge. A few yards from the bridge, a wide channel cut deep into the stone. It was edged with a bright yellow mineral deposit, and a torrent of steaming water rushed through it before dropping into the Firehole River. In other places, steam spouted out of cracks and crevices in the rock.

"Looks ghostly," Buck said. Kale nodded but didn't say anything. Buck shrugged and looked down over the railing at a trout in the clear water.

"We'll do the first shot here, Buck," Shoop called out. "You're in a good spot. Just turn this way."

As Buck turned, Shoop called out to the others. "Would you kids mind moving out of my camera's view? It will only be a minute."

"No problem," Kayla said. She tapped her brother on the shoulder. "Come on, Kale."

"Thanks," Shoop said as Toni and the twins walked off

the bridge and stood behind the tripod. "Toni, let's do a sound check."

Toni took the shotgun microphone out of its case and extended the pole. As she put on the pair of headphones, the other adults reached the bridge and stopped beside the twins.

"Of course we'll include the geothermal features that Yellowstone is famous for, but we're also interested in the wolf population," Dad was telling the Kolsons. "Half the show will be about the wolf restoration program here in the park."

Toni held the shotgun mic out toward Buck.

"There's a lot of noise from the river," she said, then turned to the adults, "and I need you guys to stop talking, please."

"No problem," Dad said, giving Toni a big smile. Then he whispered to the Kolsons, "Toni's our sound person— she's great!"

"I'll be able to filter the river noise so it won't be too loud," Shoop told Toni. "Just concentrate on Buck's voice."

Everyone was quiet as Buck looked at the camera.

When its red light came on, he smiled and said, "Welcome to Yellowstone," then looked over at Toni.

"Sounds fine," Toni said.

"Okay," Shoop said. "We're ready to roll."

"Wait a second," Dad spoke up. "Buck, take off your hoodie. You need to be filmed in your official shirt."

"I'm sorry," Buck said, pulling up the sweatshirt, exposing a T-shirt. "I don't have it on. We got up so early this morning, I just threw my hoodie on. I was going to change when we got to Old Faithful but forgot all about it when we pulled in here."

"Well, run back and—" Dad started, but Kale suddenly called out.

"Wow!" It was the first time he had spoken.

Everyone looked at Kale, then turned to follow his gaze. Upstream, a herd of bison had wandered around the bend and into the grassy meadow. There they lazily grazed in the early sun.

"Good eyes," Dad told Kale as Shoop swung the camera around.

"They look so little that far away," Toni said.

"I'm zoomed in on them," Shoop said. "It's a great shot with the water and the steam and the bison all together."

"Go put on your shirt, Buck," Dad said, handing him the keys.

"Oh man," Buck complained.

"The bison aren't going anywhere," Dad said. "You'll have plenty of time to see them when you get back."

"Bring your binoculars, too," Toni said.

Buck started back toward the Green Beast. As he walked through the empty parking spots, he peered through the forest to his right, trying to spot the bison. From his angle, he could see nothing but tree trunks. He kept trying to catch a glimpse of the beasts, but suddenly a strange noise, like a motorized mosquito, whirred past his left shoulder. Buck whipped his head around. He didn't see anything, only a white SUV pulling into a nearby parking spot. It had a set of lights across the top, a dark green stripe running along the side, and the words PARK RANGER clearly printed above the front tire.

Buck heard the whirring sound again, this time in front of him. He jerked his head around to face forward. A strange-looking bright orange plastic thing, smaller than his palm, hovered in the air a few yards away, just a little higher than his head. It looked like a four-legged spider with tiny helicopter blades spinning above each leg. A single eye in the middle of its body seemed to stare at him.

Cool, thought Buck. *A drone!*

The drone quickly zipped to the left a few feet, hovered for a second, then moved to the right. It spurted upward and dropped back down, did a little flip and hovered in front of Buck again for just a second. Then it darted across the lot toward the longer parking spaces in back. Buck was trying to keep the drone in focus when he heard Toni scream.

"Buck! Watch out!"

Buck spun around. Charging straight toward him was a wall of bison. He turned to run but took only a few steps before being tackled from the side. The breath was knocked from him, and he closed his eyes. He tried to curl up to protect himself from the onslaught of stomping hooves, but immediately something tugged at his belt. He opened his eyes and saw that a woman in a ranger uniform was pulling him into a small space of safety behind one of the boulders meant to direct traffic. The two huddled close together behind the rock as the beasts thundered past with the deafening sounds of drumming hooves and deep guttural grunts. It wasn't until the last bison had run past and the herd was slowing down at the far end of the parking lot that Buck let out his breath and relaxed his muscles.

"Are you okay?" the woman asked, her voice shaky. "I didn't think I was going to reach you in time!"

"Yeah, I'm all right," Buck said, his own voice quavering. "I didn't hear them or see them or anything until . . ." Buck reached up and wiped away a couple of tears.

"It's okay," the woman said, and squeezed his shoulder. "I was scared, too."

As they stood up, Dad, Shoop, and Toni came running across the parking lot to the rock. Dad wrapped his arms around Buck.

"I'm okay, Dad," Buck said, but buried his head into his father's shoulder. He stayed there for a few seconds, tightly hugging his dad.

"I'm okay," he repeated, stepping back and taking another swipe across his eyes with the cuff of his sweatshirt. "Thanks to . . ."

Buck looked questioningly at the woman who had rescued him.

"I'm Isabel Hodges," the woman said, smiling at Buck. "And it just dawned on me that you're the one I'm supposed to meet at Old Faithful. You're Buck Bray."

"Yeah, I am," Buck said. "And this is my dad, Dan; our cameraman, Shoop; and his daughter, Toni."

Dad extended his hand. "I don't know how to thank you," he said to Isabel. "If you hadn't been there—"

Isabel interrupted him. "Let's not even think about that. I just acted on instinct, but I'm glad I was at the right place at the right time."

"Me too!" Buck said.

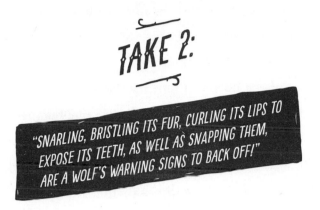

TAKE 2:

"SNARLING, BRISTLING ITS FUR, CURLING ITS LIPS TO EXPOSE ITS TEETH, AS WELL AS SNAPPING THEM, ARE A WOLF'S WARNING SIGNS TO BACK OFF!"

As the five of them stood talking, they looked across the opposite end of the parking lot at the herd. The bison were once again peacefully grazing and moving slowly away from them into the woods, but cars were streaming into the parking lot, stopping in the spaces nearest the big beasts. People started jumping out and hurrying toward the bison, cameras and phones raised.

"Excuse me. I'll be right back," Isabel said, shaking her head. "You won't believe how often this happens."

The ranger hurried over to her SUV and climbed

inside. In seconds, her voice came through a loudspeaker.

"Please stay at least seventy-five feet away from the wildlife. Bison can be extremely dangerous."

Most of the people stopped walking and stood a safe distance from the grazing animals. But one man just kept going, holding up a camera as he went.

"Sir, please return to a safe distance. You are too close," Isabel's voice called out through the loudspeaker. The man took several more steps toward the bison.

"You, sir, in the red jacket. If you don't step back, I'll have to ticket you."

The man turned and walked briskly to a car. He got in and sped away, passing between the ranger's SUV and the boulder where Buck and the others still stood.

"He probably would have listened better if he had seen them stampeding through here just a few minutes ago," Toni said as Isabel joined them again.

"People don't seem to think bison can be dangerous," Isabel said. "They look slow and clumsy, but as you saw, they can run incredibly fast. It doesn't take much to stir them up, either. Their behavior can change instantly. By the way, did anyone see what spooked them?"

"No, we were watching them graze way upstream," Toni said, "and they just suddenly started running."

"I knew they were in the meadow and were headed this way," Isabel continued. "I came to monitor them. We keep tabs on the animals in the park as much as possible. If they're close to a place where people will be, a ranger will make a presence and warn people to stay back like I just did. But there are always those who don't think the rules apply to them."

"I wasn't trying to get close to them," Buck said defensively.

"I know you weren't," Isabel reassured him.

"I was filming them," Shoop said. "Maybe we'll be able to see what set them off in the footage."

Buck looked around. "Where's your camera?"

"The Kolsons saw what happened. They offered to stay with our equipment," Shoop answered.

Buck glanced toward the bridge and saw the family standing next to Shoop's tripod. The camera was pointed straight toward him.

"Did you film the stampede?" he asked.

"I was filming the bison when they started running, and just followed them all the way to the parking lot," Shoop said. "I'm not sure what I caught after that. I was too worried about you."

"The camera is still on," Toni said. "I can see the red light."

"I'd better go turn it off," Shoop said. "It's just running down the battery."

"Go get changed, Buck," Dad said. "We'll meet you back at the bridge."

Buck glanced to the far side of the parking lot. The bison had moved deeper into the woods and were almost out of sight.

"You don't have to worry about them now," Isabel said, "but I'll come with you. I'd like to see that camper of yours."

"I wasn't worried," Buck said. "Just checking."

"I'll come, too," Toni said.

Dad and Shoop turned toward the bridge as the others headed toward the Green Beast.

"What were you looking at when I pulled in?" Isabel asked Buck.

"A little orange drone," Buck said. "It was zipping all over the place, kind of like a hummingbird, hovering here and darting there. Then it flew off in that direction." Buck pointed toward the back row of the parking lot. Now there were only two vehicles parked there, the Green Beast and the SEE AMERICA FIRST RV.

Toni quickly pulled off her backpack, took out a pamphlet, and opened it up.

"Look," she said. "It says you're not supposed to fly them in Yellowstone!"

She held the pamphlet out for Buck to see. In the corner was a small icon of a machine with four legs and four rotary blades. A red circle was drawn around the drone and a red line slashed at an angle through the middle of it. Under the icon were the words REMOTE-CONTROLLED AIRCRAFT PROHIBITED.

"We've been having a lot of trouble with those lately," Isabel said. "Another case of 'the rules don't apply to me.' Besides disturbing people and wildlife, we've actually had drones hit people, cars, and animals. One even crashed into Grand Prismatic Spring last year."

"Did they catch the guy who was flying it?" Buck asked.

"Yes, and fined him over three thousand dollars," Isabel stated. "I was hoping all the attention it got in the news would have deterred others from breaking the law. I'm not against drones; this just isn't the place to fly them. Did you happen to see who was flying the one you saw?"

"No," Buck said. "It headed toward a black pickup with a camping trailer hooked onto the back. It was parked next to our camper, but it's gone now."

Reaching the Green Beast, Buck unlocked the camper's door, and they all three stepped in.

"This is it," Toni said as Isabel glanced around the camper.

"The kitchen table turns into my bed," Buck said as he opened a small closet and pulled out a khaki-colored shirt with the show's name, THE WILD WORLD OF BUCK BRAY, embroidered in green over the pocket. "The couch in front turns into my dad's bed, and Shoop's bed folds down from above it."

"And this is my room and our schoolroom, too," Toni added. She opened one of the two doors at the back of the camper. Under a bunk bed was a desk with two computers on it. Two swivel chairs were bolted to the floor in front of the desk. "We go to school online. Mrs. Webster is our teacher."

"That's cool," Isabel said, then she looked at a sign nailed to the door. Written in big letters on the sign were the words AREA CLOSED—BEAR DANGER. Under them was a silhouette of a grizzly bear. "I like your sign. We have grizzly and black bears in Yellowstone, too."

"Toni gave me that sign at our first shoot in Denali National Park in Alaska," Buck said as he finished buttoning his official shirt. "We actually helped rescue some grizzly cubs up there."

"And this patch came from our second shoot," Toni said. She turned around to show Isabel a patch sewn onto her backpack. It had a lizard in front of a rock formation. The word CANYONLANDS was written down one side and NATIONAL PARK across the bottom. "That episode featured dinosaurs, and we got to see thousands of their tracks.

Doesn't the lizard look like a dinosaur?"

"It does," Isabel said as the three stepped from the camper. "Sounds like you two have been to some awesome places."

The two kids told Isabel about their adventures in Denali and Canyonlands as they walked back to the bridge where Dad and Shoop were waiting.

"Where are the Kolsons?" Toni asked.

"They went on across to look at Grand Prismatic," Dad said. "We'll go there as soon as we get the opening shot filmed."

"Did you have a chance to look at the footage?" Buck asked.

"Yes," Shoop answered. "We could see the big bull get irritated, but other than that, we didn't see anything unusual. Here, you guys take a look."

Isabel, Buck, and Toni watched the screen on the back of the camera. There were shots of steam coming up on the river, and then it panned over to the bison grazing far upstream. The bison didn't seem concerned about anything as they lazily lumbered along, pulling at tufts of grass.

"There's your car!" Toni said. Beyond the bison, on the far side of the meadow, was a line of spruce trees. A small image of a white SUV with the green ranger stripe could be seen through the trees as it drove past.

"The road goes right alongside the meadow," Isabel said, "just beyond those spruce trees."

"Do you think your car is what upset them?" Buck asked.

"No, they're used to vehicles," Isabel said as she watched the screen. The bison continued grazing and as the SUV drove out of sight, the camera zoomed in on the largest bull. It was standing in the middle of the others.

"This is where the big guy starts to get mad," Shoop said, looking over the others' shoulders. "See how he stops grazing and looks up for a second, then puts his head down?"

"Look how he has his tail raised," Isabel said. "That's a sign of aggravation. He's really upset."

They watched as the bull bison pawed at the ground and shook its massive head. A steamy shot of breath snorted out from its nostrils. Then the camera panned out, showing the whole herd. All the bison had become restless, and several were also pawing at the ground. Suddenly the big bull took off running, pushing past the others. Within seconds, the entire herd was charging. Shoop reached over and pushed the camera's stop button. "Did you see anything?" he asked Isabel.

"No," she said. "Maybe there wasn't anything in particular. Bison can be temperamental and unpredictable. Sometimes they just decide to run without any apparent reason."

TAKE 3:

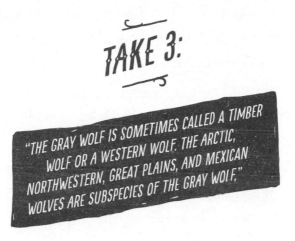

"THE GRAY WOLF IS SOMETIMES CALLED A TIMBER WOLF OR A WESTERN WOLF. THE ARCTIC, NORTHWESTERN, GREAT PLAINS, AND MEXICAN WOLVES ARE SUBSPECIES OF THE GRAY WOLF."

Buck finally stood in front of the camera wearing his official shirt. The red light on the camera came on. Dad held up a whiteboard in front of the camera with the words TAKE ONE: OPENING SHOT written on it. As soon as the board was removed, Buck started.

"Welcome to Yellowstone, the first national park in the United States," he said. "It's an amazing place of over ten thousand geothermal features such as geysers, hot springs, mud pots, and fumaroles, which are vents that release steam and gases. And do you know why Yellowstone is such a hot spot? It's the largest supervolcano in North America! But don't worry—even though it's an active volcano, it's unlikely to erupt for at least another ten thousand years."

"Great job!" Isabel said once Shoop finished filming. "I'm impressed!"

"Thanks," Buck said. "Dad makes me practice a lot."

The group gathered up their equipment, walked across the bridge, and continued along the boardwalk to Grand Prismatic Spring.

"No wonder this place is photographed so often," Toni said. "Look at the colors!" Rings of green, orange, and yellow edged the brilliant turquoise-blue water of the enormous spring. Orange and yellow rivulets trickled away from the spring, like ribbons decorating the crusty white mineral deposits that surrounded it.

"What makes all the different colors?" Buck asked Isabel.

"The water absorbs all the color rays in light except blue. The blue rays are reflected back to us, making the pools that bright aqua color," Isabel explained. "I'm going to let you guess what makes the blue change to emerald-colored water at the edges, but I'll give you a hint. Some pools are lined with yellow sulfur deposits."

"Oh, I know," Toni said. "The blue water next to the yellow deposits will make the water appear green."

"What about all the other colors?" Buck asked.

"They're made by heat-loving microorganisms called thermophiles. Different species are different colors, and they live in very specific temperature ranges," Isabel explained.

"So, the water temperature keeps getting cooler and cooler the farther out it is from the center," Buck said, "and you get those colored rings."

"Precisely," Isabel said.

"I can see why there are so many signs around telling people to stay on the boardwalks," Toni said. "It doesn't look safe to walk out there."

"It isn't," Isabel said. "A lot of what looks solid is actually a thin crust of mineral deposits. You could easily break through into boiling water underneath. In some springs, the water is deadly acidic and can eat the skin right off you. Many people have died in Yellowstone's hot springs, and hundreds seriously scalded. It's not safe at all to go off the boardwalks or designated trails."

Shoop filmed other brilliant blue pools as they continued along the boardwalk. Soon, they had looped back to the bridge. Isabel looked at her watch.

"Perfect timing," she said. "We have plenty of time to get to Old Faithful before it erupts."

As they crossed the bridge, Buck looked downstream toward the far end of the parking lot. Not a bison was in sight. Glancing upstream, he caught a glimpse of the Kolsons' RV as it drove around the bend by the meadow.

"Can Toni and I ride with you?" Buck asked Isabel.

"If that's okay with your dads."

"Sure," Dad and Shoop said in unison.

Buck and Toni climbed into the ranger's SUV. Pulling out of the parking lot, they drove past the woods, then the meadow, and it wasn't long before they turned into another parking lot.

"Wow, this is like a whole village," Toni said.

"Yes, there's a visitor center, plus hotels, restaurants,

and even a post office," Isabel said as she parked in a spot reserved for rangers.

They got out of the SUV, then met up with Dad and Shoop and headed to the area where Old Faithful could be viewed. There were several long rows of benches lined up in a huge semicircle on a wide, curving boardwalk. Beyond the boardwalk was a large area of the crusty white mineral deposits similar to what they had seen at Grand Prismatic, and in the middle was what looked like a large mound made of gray rock.

"Is that it?" Buck asked.

"Yes," Isabel said. "That mound you see is made from mineral deposits in the water left when the geyser erupts. What happens is that superheated water thousands of feet underground is forced up through cracks called fractures. This heats up groundwater that is closer to the surface of the earth. Pressure builds up as the groundwater starts to boil and steam until it is forced upward, and the geyser erupts."

"So, after an eruption," Buck said, "it starts building up pressure all over again for the next eruption, right?"

"Exactly," Isabel stated. "Sometimes that's just a few minutes later; sometimes it's years."

As Isabel spoke, people started filling the benches, staring at the mound, waiting. Shoop had his camera attached to the tripod, ready to shoot, when the Kolsons came hurrying over.

"We couldn't believe that bison stampede," Kayla said to Buck. "I would have been scared to death!" Kale didn't say anything but nodded in agreement.

"I was," Buck admitted.

"We're so glad you're okay, sweetie," Mrs. Kolson said. "I about had a heart attack watching that!"

"Let's just say I wouldn't want to repeat the experience," Buck said.

The Kolsons found a seat, and when the first puffs of steam started rising from the geyser's mouth, Buck faced the camera. Toni held the shotgun mic out toward him, and the camera's red light turned on.

"Old Faithful is beginning to put on its show," Buck recited. "It isn't the biggest geyser in Yellowstone, but it's the most famous one in the world. It faithfully erupts twenty times a day, and you can count on it to go off about every hour and a half, give or take twenty minutes. Eruptions can last up to five minutes."

As he spoke, people pointed beyond him and said *wow*. Buck turned slightly so he could watch. Water was shooting straight up in explosive spurts and mixing with steam that rapidly extended upward, rising in a massive almost mushroom-shaped cloud.

"Old Faithful can shoot water one hundred and eighty feet in the air, spewing up to eight thousand, four hundred gallons in one eruption," Buck said as he turned back to the camera. "And if you think it would make a nice sauna, think again. The water at the vent is boiling, which at this elevation is one hundred ninety-nine degrees, but the steam is over three hundred fifty degrees."

"That's a wrap," Shoop called out when the eruption finally played itself out. "Great job!"

"So, what's the plan?" Dad asked Isabel as Shoop started packing up his camera equipment. "When and where would be our best chances of seeing a wolf?"

"There are currently eleven wolf packs in the park,"

Isabel stated, "but the easiest one to watch is the Slough Creek pack in the Lamar Valley. You can actually see its den without hiking into the backcountry."

"I saw Slough Creek on the map," Toni stated. "I didn't know *slough* rhymes with *two*. I thought it was pronounced *sluff*."

Isabel laughed. "Yeah, I know what you mean. Spelling gets confusing sometimes, doesn't it? Well, anyway, the Lamar Valley is a big area in the northeast part of the park and most of the wolf packs are there."

"Are there wolves here around Old Faithful?" Buck asked. He couldn't imagine them being in an area with parking lots, buildings, and lots of people.

"The Wapiti pack was seen here last winter," Isabel said, "and made their den not too far from the Ojo Caliente Spring, about three miles north of Grand Prismatic."

"Is *Wapiti* a Native American word?" Buck asked.

"Yes, it's the Shawnee word for *elk*," Isabel stated.

"Would we be able to film the Wapiti pack, too?" Dad asked.

"No, it's not visible from the road, and because it's in

a geothermal area, it's too dangerous to walk to," Isabel said. "My office is in the visitor center. Let's go in there and I'll show you on a map. I can check to see what the spotters are reporting, too."

"What are spotters?" Buck asked.

"People that watch for and keep track of wolf activity," Isabel informed him. "Some are civilians, but the park service has spotters, too."

As the group started toward the visitor center, Shoop turned to the kids.

"Will you two take the equipment to the camper?" he asked. "We won't be shooting in the center."

"Sure," Buck said, taking Shoop's backpack.

"We'll meet you in the exhibits," Dad said, handing Buck the keys.

As Buck and Toni walked toward the Green Beast, the SEE AMERICA FIRST RV pulled out of a parking space and drove past them.

"The Kolsons seem nice," Toni said, waving at the camper as it drove away.

"Yeah, but Kale doesn't say much, does he?" Buck said.

"No," Toni said. "His sister told me he has Asperger's. She didn't say what that is, and I didn't think it was polite to ask."

"It's a mild type of autism. I used to know a kid with Asperger's," Buck said. "George Durman. He hardly ever spoke either, except about baseball. He could tell you any stat and talk about any player since baseball was invented. He didn't have many friends, but I liked George. We went to a lot of baseball games together."

They reached the Green Beast, and after putting away the equipment, they hurried to the visitor center. The two wandered around the exhibits that told how heat, water, Earth's fracture system, and earthquakes all work together to form geysers.

"Did you read this?" Toni said, looking at one of the exhibits. "Yellowstone has about two thousand earthquakes a year!"

"Wow," Buck said, just as Dad, Shoop, and Isabel came out of a nearby office.

"We'll see you early tomorrow morning," Dad said.

"I'll be at Mammoth Campground at five thirty," Isabel

said. As she headed back toward her office, Buck turned to Shoop.

"Did she mean five thirty in the *morning?*"

"Yep," Shoop answered, not sounding too pleased, either. "I guess wolves don't sleep in."

TAKE 4:

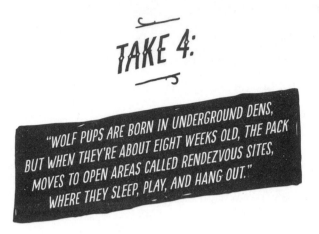

"WOLF PUPS ARE BORN IN UNDERGROUND DENS, BUT WHEN THEY'RE ABOUT EIGHT WEEKS OLD, THE PACK MOVES TO OPEN AREAS CALLED RENDEZVOUS SITES, WHERE THEY SLEEP, PLAY, AND HANG OUT."

After leaving Old Faithful, the group traveled north in the Green Beast, stopping frequently to view and film different geysers and other geothermal features. It was late afternoon when they made their last stop for the day at the Mammoth Hot Springs Terraces.

"Wow!" Buck said as they got out of the camper. "It looks like a whole hillside with layers and layers of frozen waterfalls, except they're made out of mineral deposits instead of ice."

"It says in the brochure the mineral is a type of

limestone," Toni stated.

They climbed stairs and followed boardwalks that meandered over and around the terraces. Near the top, they stopped on a deck and looked down at tiered pools of steaming water that helped form the chalky-white mineral flows.

"Is that a town down there?" Buck asked.

"Yes, that's Mammoth Hot Springs," Dad answered. "Like at Old Faithful, it has services for tourists. But it's also the headquarters for the whole park, so there are people that live there all year, too."

"I thought Mammoth was a campground," Buck said.

"Mammoth Campground is just outside of town, beyond those buildings," Dad said. "We'll be heading there as soon as we finish filming here."

It wasn't long before they were back in the Green Beast. As they wound down the hill and into town, Buck suddenly called out.

"Ice cream!" he said, looking at the Mammoth General Store, where the words were written in the window.

At the same time, Toni called out, looking in the

opposite direction.

"Elk!"

Alongside the road in a large grassy picnic area were several elk cows, their heads down, grazing. Near each of them was a young elk calf, their backs covered with white spots. Some were nursing, some standing close to their mothers, some lying in the grass.

Dad quickly guided the Green Beast to the edge of the road alongside the picnic area. Shoop rolled down the window, aiming his camera at the large brown mammals. The closest elk lifted its head for a second and then, turning, took a few steps before going back to grazing.

"Look at the light tan patches on their butts," Buck said, snapping a picture with his own camera.

"They don't seem to mind that we're here," Toni said.

"No, but there are signs everywhere that say not to approach the elk," Buck said. "I guess they come into town often."

They watched the herd graze for a few minutes, when Toni suddenly called out, "Look over there!"

Beyond the picnic area was a large red-roofed stone

building with a sign in front saying ALBRIGHT VISITOR CENTER. In the shadow of the building lay a huge elk.

"That's a big bull!" Buck exclaimed as Shoop zoomed in on it.

"Its antlers look so soft," Toni said.

"They're in velvet," Buck said. "It's a layer of fuzz that helps them grow."

"I thought they'd be a lot bigger," Toni said.

"They will be," Buck said. "A big bull like that could have antlers over four feet long by late summer when they stop growing. Then they'll shed the velvet, and the antlers will be just hard bone."

"What pamphlet did you read that in?" Toni asked.

"I didn't," Buck said. "I already knew it."

Shoop finished filming and Dad drove on, heading out of town toward the campground. Toni grabbed her pamphlets and pulled out one titled *Yellowstone Wildlife*. She opened it and read for a few seconds.

"So," she said, "I bet you an ice cream cone you don't know *when* elk shed their antlers?"

"In the spring," Buck answered.

Toni closed the pamphlet. "What flavor?"

"Chocolate," Buck answered as Dad drove down a hill and turned from the park road into the campground.

Near the campground entrance, a one-way sign and arrow indicated they needed to turn right. Dad turned and soon pulled to the side where the road widened in front of a small rustic shed. As he turned off the motor, an old man holding a small manila envelope came out of the shed and walked to Dad's window.

"Hello," Dad said. "Are you the campground host?"

"That would be me," the man replied.

"I'm Dan Bray. I believe there's a campsite reserved for us."

"Yep," the man said. "It's usually first come, first served—we don't take reservations—but Isabel made special arrangements for you. I've got number twenty-two on the lower tier marked off with cones."

"Thanks," Dad said. "Do I pay here?"

"You do," the man said. He handed the envelope to Dad. "Fill this out, and put your payment inside, please."

Like other campground envelopes Buck had seen, it

had spaces to write down the camper's name, license plate number, dates they would be staying, and which campsite they were in. As Dad wrote, the man continued talking.

"Campground quiet time is from eight p.m. to eight a.m., so no running any generators during that time," he said. "Make sure you have all food and cooking items, including water, grills, and coolers, put up either in your camper or in the provided bear box when not in use. That's my place, right there. If you have any questions or concerns, just stop by. I'm always there except when I'm not."

Chuckling at his own joke, the man pointed to an RV across the campground road with a golf cart parked in front it. An awning edged with a string of little moose-shaped lights was pulled out from one side of the RV. Beside the campsite's driveway was a post with two wooden signs hanging from hooks. One had PHILO EAST, CAMPGROUND HOST burned into it. Under it, the other sign said WELCOME ANYTIME. There was an empty hook below that.

"I like your lights, Mr. East," Toni said.

"Thank you, but call me Philo."

"Oh, your name rhymes with high-low," Buck said. "I thought it rhymed with pillow."

Philo chuckled. "A lot of people mispronounce it. I always know right off if someone knows me or not."

"Here you go," Dad said, handing Philo the envelope. "We'll be staying until Tuesday."

"Thanks. Checkout time is at ten," Philo said. He tore off the bottom half of the envelope's flap and handed it to Dad along with some other papers. "Hang this on the post at your site. And here's some info and a map of the campground. I'll be around in a little while to pick up those cones. Enjoy your stay."

"Thanks," Dad said. He handed the papers to Toni, and as he started the camper, Toni looked at the map.

The campground road made a long, one-way loop with campsites on both sides of the road. Icons indicated there were three different sets of restrooms, all of which were in the center of the loop. People camping in the lower tier would walk uphill to go to the restrooms, and those in the upper tier would walk downhill. An icon for an amphitheater was on the far end of the upper tier, and beside it was an icon of a hiker. From the hiker icon, a dotted line squiggled upward, ending with an arrow. *Trail to Mammoth* was written along the dotted line.

"Look," Toni said, showing Buck the map. "There's a trail that leads from the campground to town."

Buck looked at the map and nodded. Then he found campsite number twenty-two. "Our site is straight ahead, about halfway down on the right, Dad," he said. "It's a pull-through spot."

"Good," Dad said. "I won't have to back in."

"It's all old people camping here," Buck said as they slowly passed campsites.

"That's because school's still in session," Dad said. "Most families aren't going on vacations yet."

Soon they reached number twenty-two. Two orange cones blocked off the entrance, and two more blocked the exit at the other end. Buck and Toni jumped out and moved the first set of cones. They set them on the bench of a picnic table that was near a campfire ring. A few yards away was a big, brown metal box.

"That must be the bear box," Buck said.

As Dad pulled the Green Beast forward, Buck went over and, turning the latch, opened the two doors that swung out to the sides. Nothing was inside. He closed the doors and looked around. Several bushes and spruce trees blocked the camper from the campground road. More bushes and trees were at the sides of the site, giving privacy from the neighboring campsites. Beyond the campsite to the east there was a strip of land about fifty feet wide, covered in clumps of sagebrush and sprinkled with dots of early blooming wildflowers among tufts of scruffy grasses. It ran the entire length of the campground and was bordered on the other side by the main park road. Beyond the road, scrubby hills rose up to meet a line of tall cliffs. On the left of the wide canyon, even taller mountains rose far in the distance, their tops still covered with snow.

"I wonder where that goes," Buck said to Toni. Across the main road, a quarter of a mile to their right, was a barren hill. A well-worn path went to the top. Railroad ties were placed every few feet, fending off erosion and making steps.

"I don't know," Toni said, "but look. There's another trail down there."

A quarter of a mile to their left was another hill. A paved pull-off area on the side of the road was near the hill's base. A wooden sign stood at the edge of a trail that wrapped around the bottom of the hill and disappeared as it headed toward the towering cliffs beyond.

Buck put his binoculars to his eyes. "It looks like a trailhead sign, but I can't read it from this angle. I bet Philo knows where the trails go," Buck said. He turned to his father, who now stood beside the camper, stretching as he also looked around. "Hey, Dad, can we take the cones back to Philo and then explore the campground?"

"Sure, but I don't want you going over there," Dad said, pointing across the road to the hill with the wooden steps. "Stay in the campground. We'll have supper in about an hour."

"Okay," Buck said. He hurried to the end of their driveway and picked up the two cones. Toni grabbed the two from the picnic table, and they headed up the campground road, stopping when they reached the shed. Philo was at his campsite, sitting in a camp chair under the awning. His head was bent over some sort of device in his hand.

"Hey, Philo," Buck called out across the road. "Where do you want these?"

Philo looked up and, seeing the kids, got to his feet and set the device on the picnic table. "Hey, thanks for bringing those back—saves me a trip," he said, walking toward the kids. "We'll put them in the shed."

Philo unlocked the shed door and stacked the cones inside. As he snapped the lock closed again, Buck asked, "Where does that trail with the steps go?"

"Just up and over the hill," Philo answered. "On the other side is a small residential area where some of the park workers live. You can't see the houses from the campground; the hill hides them. But you can from up on top, plus, a good view of the whole canyon."

"What about that other hill?" Toni said. "It looks like there's a trail marker sign down by a pull-off."

"There is," Philo said. "It's the trailhead for quite a few

trails. You can get down to the Gardner River on one of them. The river runs down through this canyon and flows into the Yellowstone River, about five miles down, just before the park boundary."

The three chatted for a few minutes, Buck and Toni explaining to Philo about their TV show. Then the two kids headed back down the campground road. When they got to their site, they kept on walking, peering into each campsite they passed.

"They all have bear boxes," Buck said.

"And some people are using them," Toni said. "Some have locks on the latches. I wonder if we'll see a bear in our campsite."

"It's not a bear, but look!" Buck said, stopping. Farther down an elk had walked out from behind some junipers and paused in the middle of the campground road.

"Isn't it beautiful?" Toni said.

Buck looked at it through his binoculars. He handed them to Toni, then he pulled out his camera from a pocket in his cargo pants and took a shot.

"I zoomed in, but it was too far away to get a good

shot," he said, showing Toni the picture.

They watched the elk as it continued into a campsite, walking past someone's RV. It stopped for a few seconds, pulling a few leaves from a bush, then continued on across the scruffy strip of land toward the main road, stopping occasionally to grab at a few tufts of grass. It crossed the road, passed the trailhead sign, and started following the trail toward the Gardner River.

"That was awesome," Buck said when it was out of sight. "I wonder if we'll have any animals wander through our campsite."

"That would be cool," Toni said as they started walking again. Soon they reached the end of the lower tier, and the road curved uphill to their left.

"Let's find the trail to Mammoth," Buck said as they headed upward.

"We're not supposed to leave the campground," Toni said.

"We won't. We'll just see where it starts," Buck said.

"You always say that, and then we end up getting into—" Toni stopped short. "Look! The Kolsons!"

At the last campsite before the road curved left again sat a SEE AMERICA FIRST RV.

"How do you know?" Buck argued. "We've seen a lot of those rental campers."

"Because there's Kayla and Kale." Toni pointed to two kids high on the hill behind the campsite.

"Hey, Kayla, Kale!" she yelled out, and waved.

"Come on up," Kayla hollered back. "There's a trail at the amphitheater."

"Okay," Toni yelled, but Buck looked at her.

"So, *now* it's okay to leave the campground?" he said, grinning.

Toni ignored him and took off running. Buck was right on her heels. They ran past the Kolsons' campsite and curved onto the upper tier, where there was a small parking area and a sign that said AMPHITHEATER. A short path led to several rows of benches in front of a stage with an outdoor movie screen. Toni slowed down, but Buck saw a sign to the side of the stage that said TRAIL TO MAMMOTH, and raced passed her.

Toni followed. The path soon turned rocky and steep,

forcing the two to stop running. They continued to climb, but it wasn't long before they could see Kayla and Kale again. The two were sitting on a wooden bench beside a sharp bend in the trail.

"This is cool!" Buck said. Kayla and Kale scooted over, letting Buck and Toni sit down, too. "You can see the whole campground from up here."

"Yeah, we saw you guys pull in," Kayla said. "I thought for sure you'd climb that hill with the steps, didn't I, Kale?"

"We bet," he said. "Kayla owes me an ice cream cone."

"Really?" Buck said. "Toni owes me one, too."

"Chocolate," Kale said.

"Me too!" Buck said, then looked the opposite way, where beyond the bend, the trail rose even more steeply. "Did you walk all the way up to Mammoth to get one?"

"No, when we got here, our parents said it was too late," Kayla answered. "Maybe we could all go together tomorrow."

"That would be fun if we're back in time," Toni said. "We're going to look for wolves tomorrow."

"Cool," Kayla said.

"Are you here on vacation?" Buck asked. "You're the only kids we've seen in the campground."

"No," Kale said.

"Kale's in a drone competition," Kayla said.

"Really?" Buck said. "You can have drones here?"

"No," Kale said. Buck noticed Kale often answered only exactly what was asked without elaborating. However, his sister explained.

"The competition isn't in the park. It's at a school in Gardiner—a little town just outside the park's northern entrance," Kayla said. "Kale loves flying drones and has been in a bunch of competitions. When he qualified for this one, my parents thought we should see Yellowstone while we were here."

Buck turned to Kale. "I was looking at a little drone when the bison charged. Did you see it?"

Kale shook his head, but his sister gave him a nudge, and he added, "How big?"

"Really little—smaller than my hand."

"What color?" Kale said.

"Orange."

"An OR-213 quadcopter," Kale said.

"What's a quadcopter?" Toni asked.

"A drone with four rotors," Kale answered. When Kale didn't explain further, Toni looked questioningly at Kayla.

"Like blades on a helicopter," Kayla said.

"Do you have an OR-213?" Buck asked Kale.

"Yes," Kale answered.

"Do you have it here?" Buck asked.

"No," Kale said.

"Kale, you're supposed to give more complete answers," his sister reprimanded.

"No," Kale repeated, "not here. In the RV."

"Is that what you'll fly in the competition tomorrow?" Toni asked.

"No," Kale said.

Kale said no more, so Kayla piped in again. "He brings the OR-213 with him everywhere, but he flies a bigger drone for the competition."

"Well, I know you weren't the one flying the OR-213 I saw," Buck said. "You were with Toni when that happened."

Suddenly a woman's voice could be heard from below. "Kayla, Kale, time for dinner."

They all looked down. Mrs. Kolson was standing beside their RV, waving up to them.

"Be right down," Kayla called out.

Walking in single file, Kale followed Buck as he led the way down the trail. As usual, Kale said nothing and Buck joined Kale in his silence, but the two girls talked the entire way. When they reached the campground road, they stopped.

"I guess we'll see you around," Buck said to the twins. "We're going across the upper tier so we can see the entire campground."

Toni took off her backpack and brought out a sketchpad. She quickly wrote something down and tore off the corner of the page.

"Here're our dads' phone numbers," she said, handing Kayla the scrap of paper. "Call us if you hike into town to get ice cream. Maybe we'd be able to go with you."

"I'll give you my mom's number," Kayla said. As she wrote, a black pickup towing a camping trailer came around the bend and zoomed past them.

"I'm a droner," Kale suddenly said.

"We know you are," his sister said patiently.

"No," Kale said, "he is." He pointed to the back of the trailer as it drove away from them. Saying nothing more, Kale headed toward his campsite.

Kayla shrugged. "He probably knows them. He sees a lot of the same people at different competitions," she offered in explanation. Then, saying goodbye, she followed her brother downhill toward their RV.

TAKE 5:

"A WOLF HAS A FANTASTIC SENSE OF SMELL. IT CAN DETECT PREY BY SMELL UP TO 1.75 MILES AWAY."

Buck and Toni headed the opposite direction, walking in the middle of the road as it gradually went uphill along the upper tier.

"We probably should have asked the Kolsons to come wolf watching with us," Toni said.

"I doubt Dad would like that," Buck said. "You know how he is on a shoot. All work and no fooling around."

"You're the one who is usually fooling around," Toni said. "Like at the Artists' Paintpots this afternoon. We had to shoot that mud pot scene three times because of you."

"I liked the sounds the bubbling mud made as it splurted and splattered," Buck said. *"Blup, bloo-bloop, blurp. Blu-blu-blu, bloop-bloop, blurp."*

Toni rolled her eyes. "I shouldn't have brought it up again."

"It was almost like a bunch of toads were hiding in there just under the surface, burping and belching," Buck said. "I couldn't help trying to imitate them."

"Your dad didn't think it was funny. And it smelled when you burped."

"I didn't burp on purpose on the second shoot. All that air I swallowed just sort of came out."

"Well, it stunk."

"The steam from that fumarole smelled worse."

"Yeah, like rotten eggs," Toni agreed, wrinkling her nose as she remembered the sulfuric smell.

A grin spread over Buck's face. He gulped a couple of times, then opened his mouth and let out a big, long belch.

"Stop it!" Toni said. She reached out to playfully hit him, but Buck took off running. Toni chased after him.

They were almost at the end of the upper tier when Buck stopped.

"Look," he said. "There's where that guy Kale recognized is camping."

Backed into the driveway of the last campsite was the black pickup, the camping trailer still attached behind it.

"I get it!" Buck suddenly exclaimed. "I'm a droner!"

"What are you talking about?" Toni said.

"Kale didn't recognize the guy. He wouldn't have even been able to see him inside those dark-tinted windows," Buck said. "He was reading the license plate!"

Toni looked at the blue-and-white plate on the pickup. The tag read 1MA-DRNR.

"Do you get it?" Buck said impatiently. "The number one could be a read as an *I*, making the words *I'm a*. The rest is *droner* without the vowels."

"Oh, I see!" Toni said.

"You know what? That little drone I saw at Grand Prismatic—what did Kale call it? An OR-213?" Buck said, and Toni nodded. "It was heading back to a black pickup with a camping trailer."

"Did you notice its license plate number?" Toni asked.

"No, but it had a camper shell over the truck bed, and all the windows were tinted, just like this one."

"Maybe it will be in Shoop's video," Toni said. "Come on, let's go look."

The two took off running but had only taken a few steps when Buck suddenly stopped and spun around.

"Did you hear that?" he asked, his head twisting back and forth, his eyes searching.

"Hear what?" Toni said.

"Listen."

A slight breeze rippled the pale green leaves of quaking aspen trees. A raven cawed in the distance, and the thud of a hatchet splitting firewood echoed from somewhere in the campground below.

"I don't hear anything," Toni said.

"It was a mechanical whirling sound, just like that drone made at Grand Prismatic."

"Do you still hear it?" Toni asked.

"No. I only heard it for a second, and then it stopped."

The two scanned the four nearby campsites. In the

site just below the black pickup sat an RV with a light on inside. An older woman could be seen through open blinds as she prepared dinner. A man was also inside, reading a paper. Across the road from that RV, a man was setting up a tent near another black pickup with a shell. It, too, had dark-tinted windows in both the cab and the truck bed shell. And at the site just above it, a woman was holding the hand of a redheaded toddler as a man climbed out of a pop-up camper that sat in the bed of a gold pickup.

"Look!" the woman called out to her husband. She quickly picked up the child and pointed beyond the man setting up the tent. Buck immediately searched the air for a drone.

"Do you see it, Tucker?" the woman said. "It's a moose!"

Buck's eyes dropped to where the woman pointed. A young, gangly-legged moose was walking through a vacant campsite farther down the road.

"Cool!" Toni said as Buck whipped his camera out of his pocket. He snapped several pictures as they watched the moose amble down the hillside. The clumsy-looking creature easily stepped over clumps of sagebrush and pushed through clusters of pine and aspen trees. Then, unexpectedly, it took off running and went out of sight behind one of the restrooms.

"That was neat," Buck said to Toni. "At first I thought that kid's mom had seen a drone."

"Me too," Toni said, "but I don't see anybody flying one up here."

"No, but I'm almost positive I heard one," Buck said.

The two hurried on around the bend. At the bottom of the hill, they turned toward the registration area.

"Look!" Buck said as they jogged passed Philo's signpost.

Now hanging below the sign that read WELCOME ANYTIME was another sign that said BUT NOT NOW!

"That's hysterical," Toni said, laughing.

When they got to their campsite, a golf cart was parked behind the Green Beast. Philo was heading toward Buck's father, who stood by the grill, a spatula in his hand. As Dad took the last hamburger patty off the fire and put it on a plate, Shoop stepped out of the camper's door. He had a bag of hamburger buns, a bottle of ketchup, and a jar of pickles in one hand, a bag of lettuce and a bottle of salad dressing in the other. A bag of chips was held between his teeth. He leaned over the table and, opening his mouth, let the bag of chips drop.

"Your timing is always perfect," Shoop said to Buck and Toni. He then looked over at Philo. "Yours too! Care to join us for dinner? We've got plenty if you get to it before Buck does!"

"Hey, I'm growing!" Buck defended himself as the others laughed.

"Well, I didn't come for dinner," Philo said. "I came to give you some news I think you'll be pretty interested in, but I wouldn't mind having a bite."

Toni ran into the Green Beast for another plate, and as they started eating, Dad turned to Philo. "So, what was the news you were going to tell us?"

"Seems we have a killer in the park," Philo said.

Everyone stopped eating and stared at the man.

"What?" Buck, Toni, Shoop, and Dad all said simultaneously in alarm.

"Earlier this afternoon, one of the rangers found a dead

coyote alongside the road," Philo reported. "At first, he thought it had been hit by a car, but then he saw a second dead coyote a few yards away."

"Were they shot?" Buck asked.

"I don't know," Philo said. "I didn't hear a lot of details."

"How did you hear?" Dad asked.

"I have a radio scanner and can listen in on communications between rangers," Philo explained. "I usually listen on and off all day, but I was pretty busy today and didn't have it on until this evening."

"Can we go back to your place and listen now?" Buck asked.

"No, the batteries died while I was listening," Philo said. "That's why I don't know much. They take several hours to recharge, so I'll have to wait until tomorrow to do that. It wouldn't be right for the campground host to run a generator during quiet time."

"I'm sure we'll find out more when Isabel gets here tomorrow," Dad said.

"Well, I'd better go for my last check around the campground for the night," Philo said, getting up from the table. "Thanks for dinner, and good luck tomorrow. I hope you see some wolves."

They said their goodbyes, and as Philo drove away, Buck turned to Shoop. "Can Toni and I watch the video from Grand Prismatic again?"

"Sure," Shoop answered. "While you two were exploring the campground, I saved a backup on a thumb drive. It's in my camera case. You can watch it on one of your computers."

"Thanks!" Buck said.

"Don't fool around too long," Dad said. "And if you have any homework, you need to send it to Mrs. Webster. We have to get to bed early, too. We need to be up by five."

"Okay," Buck groaned.

Toni got the thumb drive and, sitting at their desk, opened up the video on her computer. She fast-forwarded and then paused the video once the bison had all gone past Buck and Isabel, but the two were still beside the rock. Then she zoomed in. Buck and Toni looked carefully at a pixelated image of a black pickup with a trailer parked next to the Green Beast. Buck took the mouse and moved the image until the license plate took up most of the computer screen.

"That's it!" he exclaimed.

"It's the same color," Toni said, "but it's kind of hard to tell if it says *I'm a droner*. It's too pixelated."

"I think it does. The second letter is definitely an *M*," Buck insisted. "And even though it's hard to tell whether those are *R*s or *K*s, there are two of them and they're in the right places, fifth letter and last."

"I'm not convinced," Toni said.

Buck zoomed out until the pickup became less pixelated, but then the license plate was too small to determine anything.

"We better see if we have any homework," Toni said. She closed out of the video, pulled out the thumb drive, and set it on the desk. Then she went online, bringing up their school site.

"Yep, lots of homework," she said. "Mostly math—metrics, to be exact."

"I'm going to download the pictures I took of the elk

and moose first," Buck said. He opened a desk drawer, pulled out a cable, stuck one end into a USB port on his own computer and the other in his camera.

"That's a good one," he said. "I caught the moose just as it started running."

Toni looked over at his screen.

"Whoa, wait a second," she said. Grabbing Buck's mouse, Toni zoomed in. "Look!"

In the air, a few feet above the moose's head, was something orange.

"An OR-213!" Buck exclaimed. "That's why the moose suddenly started running!"

"You don't think Kale was flying it, do you?" Toni said.

Buck didn't answer. Instead he grabbed the mouse back from Toni, put the thumb drive in his computer, and brought up Shoop's video. He fast-forwarded until he reached the first shots of the bison grazing in the distance. Pausing when the big bull became agitated, he zoomed in and put his face closer to the screen.

"What are you doing?" Toni said.

"Looking," Buck replied. "The moose started running

because of an OR-213. It could have been Kale's, or it could have been someone else's. I don't know. But maybe the bison started running because of one, too." Buck looked at the screen carefully as he moved the image around, zooming in and out.

"Look at this! It's not an OR-213, but it's definitely something." Buck zoomed out to the original image. "Keep looking right there."

He pointed to a particular spruce among the trees that lined the road. Isabel's white SUV could be seen behind it, and in the foreground stood the massive bull bison, steam coming from its nostrils.

Toni peered closely at the screen, and Buck zoomed in. The image became more and more pixelated until the spruce and the SUV consisted only of small squares in various shades of green and white. They no longer looked like a tree and a vehicle. But there were also some gray pixels.

"Is that what you're talking about?" Toni asked. "That gray shape?"

"Yes, and that little bit of red," Buck answered.

"It does look different from the trees and the car," Toni admitted. "The gray looks almost like a bow with four loops."

"I think it's a drone," Buck said. "A gray one and much bigger than an OR-213. I think those loops are the protective plastic loops that go around the rotors. I don't know what the red is."

"I guess it could be a drone," Toni said. "But it could be something else. It's really too pixelated to tell."

"Yeah, but watch," Buck said.

Buck zoomed back out, and the pixelated squares started turning back into tree branches. Now only a small shadow of gray could be seen. Buck turned off the pause, and the video started playing. Just a fleeting glimpse of a gray shadow, looking almost like the steam from the bison's breath, moved toward the bull bison for only a second. Then it disappeared behind the animal's massive body. Buck pushed pause again, just as the bison pawed the ground and shook its huge head.

"I'm sure that was a drone," Buck exclaimed, "and it made the bison stampede!"

TAKE 6:

"HEADLINE NEWS! WOLVES HELP MAKE A HEALTHIER ENVIRONMENT! SINCE THE WOLF'S REINTRODUCTION, THE NUMBER OF BEAVER COLONIES IN YELLOWSTONE HAS GONE FROM ONE TO NINE."

FRIDAY, MAY 16

Buck tossed and turned, not able to get to sleep. He was convinced that a drone had set off the stampede. He was also convinced that the person with the 1MA-DRNR license plate had something to do with it.

"Couldn't have," Toni had said earlier when she was doing her homework. "That truck was there in the parking lot already. You were watching the OR-213 go toward it when the bison started charging. Whoever owns that truck couldn't be in two places at the same time."

Buck knew she was right. And, when he had shown

Dad and Shoop the video, they hadn't felt like the bit of gray shadow was a drone at all.

"A piece of dust on a lens can make a weird shadow," Shoop had said, and before they went to bed, Shoop carefully cleaned all his lenses.

Buck closed his eyes. It had begun to rain and the drops on the camper's roof finally lulled him to sleep. The next thing he knew, Dad was shaking him awake. Buck quickly dressed and went outside. It had stopped raining. Stars were out and the air was chilly. He hurried to the campground restroom. When he returned, his bed was turned back into a table, and Dad was pouring steaming oatmeal into bowls. They had barely finished eating when Philo knocked on the door.

"Isabel's parked up by my place," he said when Buck opened the door. "She didn't want to wake everyone up driving through the campground. I told her I'd come down with my cart and help haul your equipment up there."

"What happened to your hand?" Buck asked. Philo's index and middle fingers were wrapped together with several bandages, and his hand below the fingers was swollen and purple.

"Oh, I buggered it up last night helping a camper lift a generator," Philo said. "I thought it was kind of weird that he would have a generator, since he's tent camping, but he said he had a lot of electronics he had to keep charged up."

"Did you see a doctor?" Dad said, looking at Philo's fingers. "They could be broken."

"I think they are," Philo said. "The clinic in Mammoth was already closed when it happened, so I just doctored it up myself. I'll try to get up there today."

Buck and Toni helped their fathers put the equipment and a cooler filled with sandwiches and water into the back of the cart. Then they jumped in beside Philo. Philo said he would come back for Dad and Shoop, but they told him they'd just walk up.

As Philo made a U-turn and headed in the wrong direction up the one-way campground road, Buck asked, "What's the name of the guy camping in the last site? He's got a black pickup."

"Lyall Griffith," Philo said. "He's the guy with the

generator."

"No, the guy across the road from him," Buck said. "He has a black pickup and a camping trailer."

"Let me think. I talk with everyone when they register, but it's hard to remember who's camping where," Philo answered. He drove on for a few seconds before speaking again. "It may be the Roberts. A young couple with a toddler."

"No," Toni said. "They have a gold pickup."

"Hmmm," Philo said, scratching his head. "I'll look it up."

Philo pulled the golf cart in front of the shed, and they all went in. Philo turned on the light, then he picked up a small box filled with camper registration envelopes and pulled out the one in the back.

"Oh yeah," he said. "Steve Dekster and his son, Jason. I remember them. Jason is fifteen—just got his learner's permit to drive. He's here for the drone competition in Gardiner tomorrow. There's another droner here, also. A boy about your age. Has a sister, too."

"That's Kale and Kayla Kolson. We've met them," Toni stated.

Philo locked the shed, and they drove across the road to where Isabel was parked next to Philo's welcome sign.

"Good morning," Isabel said. "What's going on?"

"We were wondering about a kid camping here named Jason Dekster," Toni said. "Buck thinks he's the one who was flying the OR-213 at Grand Prismatic."

"And we know someone was chasing a moose with one here in the campground, too," Buck added.

"OR-213?" Isabel asked, then quickly continued. "Oh, you mean the little orange drone you were watching."

"Yeah," Buck said. "It flew toward a truck with the same license plate number as the Deksters' truck."

"Actually, Buck *thinks* it was the same number," Toni corrected, "but we couldn't tell for sure. It was too pixelated on the video."

"We also *think*," Buck added, rolling his eyes at Toni, "that there was a drone in the spruce trees near the bison when they started charging. Something looked kind of like a drone in Shoop's video."

Shoop and Dad walked up and heard what Buck was saying.

"I think Buck is letting his imagination get away from him," Dad said. "Shoop says there was probably a speck of dust on the lens."

Buck ignored his father and spoke again to Isabel. "When you were driving to Grand Prismatic, did you see anybody near those spruce trees by the road?"

"There were a few vehicles parked alongside the road up there, but people are always stopping to watch animals, so I didn't think much of it," Isabel said. "But, even if you did see a drone in the video, it would be pretty hard to prove anything without catching someone red-handed."

"Well, we might not be able to prove who," Buck said, "but we know someone was pestering a moose with a drone here in the campground yesterday."

"Well, if we catch him, he'll get a pretty hefty fine," Isabel said. "Up to five thousand dollars, and possibly time in jail, especially if he is disturbing or chasing wildlife. That's illegal in the entire state of Wyoming."

"I'll chat with all the campers a bit this morning, just reminding them about the rules," Philo said.

"And keep your eyes peeled for any unidentified flying

objects," Buck said. They said goodbye to Philo and piled into Isabel's SUV. With Buck and Toni in front, and Shoop and Dad in back, Isabel drove up the hill to Mammoth.

"So, what can you tell us about the coyotes found dead near the road?" Dad asked as they turned east toward the Lamar Valley.

"How did you hear about that?" Isabel replied.

"Philo said he heard about it on his radio scanner."

Isabel chuckled. "Good old Philo. He probably knows more about what's going on in this park than anyone. What did he tell you?"

"Not much," Toni said. "His batteries died before he heard any details."

"Were the coyotes shot?" Buck asked.

"No," Isabel said. "We think they were poisoned."

"Poisoned?" all four passengers asked.

"We *think*," Isabel said. "They're going to do an autopsy today to find out. Both coyotes looked to be in perfectly good health, and there wasn't a mark on them, so we know they weren't shot or hit by a car. We're actually hoping they got into some poison someplace by accident, but there's always the possibility that a person poisoned them."

"Why would someone want to poison them?" Toni asked.

"There are some people who aren't too fond of coyotes," Isabel stated. "And they're even less fond of wolves. Both species have been known to kill sheep and other livestock on nearby ranches. You can legally hunt coyotes and wolves in all three states surrounding Yellowstone—Wyoming, Montana, and Idaho—but there's a lot of controversy about whether wolves should even be here."

"Why?" Buck asked. "Wolves are a native species."

"Yes," Isabel answered. "Wolves were here before settlers came and built farms and ranches, but those wolves were totally eradicated in this area. The last wolf in Yellowstone was killed in 1926."

"That's horrible," Toni said.

"I think it is, too," Isabel stated. "But back then, people didn't know a lot about ecosystems and biodiversity and how things in nature are interconnected. They saw the wolf only as a predator. In 1995, though, wolves were reintroduced into Yellowstone."

"They brought them in from Canada," Buck stated. "I learned that for one of our scripts."

"That's right," Isabel said. "We've been studying them ever since, discovering so much about how a top predator affects ecosystems."

They drove along, watching as the landscape became visible with the growing sunlight. Soon, Isabel turned into a pull-off and stopped.

"Is this where we might see wolves?" Buck asked, picking up the binoculars hanging around his neck. He quickly scanned the meadow. A stream flowed down the middle. At the far end was some marshy wetland with reeds and cattails. Beyond them willows lined the banks of a small pond.

"No, but this is a perfect example of how the wolf affected an ecosystem," Isabel said. "Once, this valley was overgrazed by elk, so much so that the grass was eaten down to almost nothing. The marsh was there, but that pond wasn't. When the wolves were reintroduced, they fed on the weak and diseased elk, making the herd stronger. The elk learned not to stay out in the open as much, which meant the grasses had more chance to grow, giving all sorts of smaller mammals and birds things to eat. Over time, bigger plants grew, like those willows, which brought beaver. The beaver made dams, forming that pond, which brought even more animals, such as moose, fish, insects, and amphibians. The biodiversity here now is just amazing. And we can thank the wolf, in part, for that."

While Isabel was talking, Shoop had rolled down the window and filmed the meadow.

"I got that all recorded," he said when Isabel stopped talking. "Both audio and video. Do you mind if we use your voice in that shot?"

"That would be awesome!" Isabel stated. "I've never been on TV before, even if it's just my voice!"

They pulled out onto the road again, winding around sagebrush-covered hills dotted with stands of aspen, spruce, pine, and juniper. They marveled at sparkling streams rushing with spring snowmelt and were awed by waterfalls cascading over cliffs. They crossed the Yellowstone River, the bridge spanning high above the river's canyon. They had just reached the far side of the bridge when Buck suddenly called out.

"Look!"

Isabel quickly pulled to the shoulder of the road as three bighorn sheep scrambled up a rocky cliff on the opposite side. Throughout the drive, Shoop had his camera ready, asking Isabel to pull over so he could take a sweeping shot of meadow wildflowers, video the mirror image of a snowcapped mountain reflecting in a pond, or record a bald eagle they spied preening in a tree. Buck also had his camera ready. He had snapped a photograph of a black bear with twin cubs that he briefly glimpsed as they drove through an area of deep woods. But now, as they both tried to capture these fleet-footed grayish-brown creatures with white rumps and curved horns, a pickup zoomed around them, blocking the sheep from sight. Once the truck was past, the sheep were gone, too.

"Darn," Buck said, looking at the screen on his camera. "I missed them. All I got were two shots of that truck."

"That's all I got, too," Shoop stated.

"Hold on, we might get lucky," Isabel said, putting the SUV in gear and quickly pulling back onto the road. She drove up a steep bend, made a sharp left onto a dirt road, then quickly stopped and turned off the motor.

"See that drop-off? They'll probably come right up over it," Isabel said. Beyond a wide area of grass and sagebrush, the top half of some junipers could be seen, but beyond them, nothing but air. Shoop aimed the camera out the window. Buck held his camera ready, too. Within seconds, the bighorn sheep scrambled up over the edge and started grazing in the grass. Each had thick, wide horns that curved back from the top of their heads and circled forward until the ends were even with their cheeks.

"Those are all rams. They hang out together in bachelor groups," Isabel stated. "Ewes will have more narrow horns that curve back in only a short arc."

"Awesome," Toni whispered. "We're so close. Glad you knew this road was here."

"I've seen them up here before," Isabel whispered. "They hang out on the cliffs above the Yellowstone River but will come up here to graze. That one is about the biggest ram I've ever seen. You can tell how old it is by counting the rings on its horns."

Buck put his camera on his lap and picked up the binoculars.

"He's our age," he said quietly to Toni. He slipped the binoculars from his neck and handed them to her.

"They're so shabby," Toni said.

"They're losing their winter coats," Isabel explained.

The sheep grazed, seemingly unaware that they were being watched. Then, suddenly, at the sound of a vehicle on the main road, they darted over the edge and were instantly gone from sight.

"That's why I like to get out early in the morning," Isabel said. "It's when you'll see the most wildlife."

TAKE 7:

"GRAY WOLF IS THE NAME OF THE SPECIES, BUT ITS FUR CAN BE GRAY, BLACK, WHITE, OR A COMBINATION OF THESE MIXED WITH TAN."

They drove on, but it wasn't long before they turned onto another dirt road. Coming around a bend, they saw a line of vehicles parked along one side and a group of people in the grass on the other. Beyond them an open sagebrush-covered hillside dropped steeply away to a creek far down at the bottom. On the other side of the creek, another hill rose steeply, and beyond, even more hills.

"This is Slough Creek," Isabel said as she pulled up behind a car and turned off the motor. "And those are the spotters."

Buck looked through the eyepiece. "Oh, I see," he said. "It's like they have a dirt patio out in front." He stepped back, and as he let Toni have a turn, he looked through his binoculars.

"I can't find it now," he said.

"Put them down for a second," Lobo said, coming over to stand beside Buck. "Just look with your eyes. See way out there, a little to the right. There's a dead tree trunk. The only one around."

"Yeah, I see it," Buck said. Toni lifted her head and looked as well.

"Okay, with the binoculars, find that tree. Then move your eyes up the hillside and a little to the left. There's an old bison skull, bleached white." Both Buck and Toni followed his directions.

"Got it," Buck said.

"Now move slowly on upward from the skull, and you should be able to make out the dark hole and the lighter patio."

"I found it!" Toni stated.

"I see it, too!" Buck said. "Not as clear as with the scope, but I'm sure I'd be able to see a wolf if one came out."

"Oh, you will." Lobo laughed. "It's not *if* one comes out, it's *when.*"

As they looked through the binoculars, Dad and Shoop each took a peek through Isabel's scope and then announced they were going to get set up.

"We'll be down there a ways," Shoop said. "Away from the others so we don't have to worry about sound interference."

"You kids can keep watching here until we're ready," Dad said. As he and Shoop walked away, Lobo turned to Isabel and Toni.

"If you two will keep an eye on the den," he said, "Buck and I will get us all something warm to drink."

Toni put her eye to the spotting scope, while Buck followed Lobo to the table. As they filled cups with steaming coffee and hot chocolate, the two talked.

"Nothing's happening yet," Toni said when they returned. As the four sipped their drinks, one of them always kept an eye to the scope. They had barely finished their refreshments, when Dad came back.

"Okay, kids. We're ready," he said.

"Can't we wait so we can see the wolves come out?" Buck complained.

"We want to shoot you before they come out so Shoop can focus on the wolves when they do appear," Dad said, then he turned to Lobo. "How much longer do you think it will be?"

"Who knows?" Lobo said. "Could be five seconds, could be an hour. But they will come out sooner or later, and once they do, they'll be out for a while. You won't miss seeing them."

"Okay." Buck relented and walked away with his father. Toni started to follow, but Isabel stopped her.

"Won't Shoop want Buck in the foreground when the wolves are out?" Isabel asked.

"No, he'll film Buck separately, then edit and splice it all together later," Toni answered. "Shoop's amazing. It will probably end up looking like Buck is standing right in front of the den."

Toni ran to where Shoop had his camera mounted on a tripod and aimed toward the den. Dad positioned Buck with his back to the far hillside. Toni put on the headphones, took the shotgun microphone from its case, and had Buck say a line to check the sound.

"Good to go," she announced, and the red light on the camera turned on.

"Just a second," Buck said to Shoop, and the light went off. Buck looked at his father.

"Dad," he said, a tinge of nervousness in his voice.

"What's the matter?" his father asked.

"Nothing," Buck said, "but I need to tell you. I'm going to ad-lib a bit in this shot, not say everything I rehearsed."

"Buck, just say your lines," Dad said sternly. "I don't want any more fooling around, like you did yesterday."

"Believe me, Dad, I won't mess it up. I just learned a lot from Lobo. Stuff we didn't know to put into the script."

Dad sighed but didn't say any more. He took the whiteboard with *Take 7: Wolf Scene* written on it and held it in front of his son. The camera's red light turned on again, and Dad stepped away.

"I'm here at Slough Creek," Buck said, "but I'm not the only one here. Behind me, high on that other hillside, is a den with three wolf pups and their mother inside." Buck paused for a second, knowing Shoop would later splice a close-up of the den into the videoed scene.

"Here in Yellowstone, wolves are officially identified by a number such as 624M, the *M* standing for *male*." Buck continued, "But often, as the case is here, they are unofficially given names by the spotters who come to wolf watch."

Shoop put up his hand, indicating he wanted Buck to pause again. Buck knew Shoop would splice in a shot of all the spotters lined up watching once a wolf was seen. When Shoop nodded, Buck continued.

"In the Slough Creek pack, there are seven wolves. The alpha male is a huge gray wolf called Odin. The alpha female is Jord. She's black with a small white triangle on her chest. This spring Jord had three wolf pups. They haven't been given names yet but are referred to by their colors—light gray, black, and two-toned, which is gray on the back and head with light tan legs. Also in this pack are two subordinate females called Geri and Freki, both two-toned. They are like doting aunts who watch over and play with the pups but also help bring food back to the den. If you keep your eye on that small dark hole on that far hill, it won't be long before you'll see these spectacular creatures, which are named after a god, his wife, and their two wolf pets from Norse mythology."

Buck stopped talking, waited a few seconds, and then pulling his finger across his throat, said, "Cut." The red light on Shoop's camera went out.

"Wow," Dad said, smiling. "You did great!"

"Thanks," Buck replied, beaming.

"That info about the wolves' names was super," Dad said. "I'm sorry I doubted you."

"That's okay," Buck said, but he didn't have time to say anything more.

"I see a head!" Lobo's voice called out. "It's looking out of the den!"

The spotters all hurried to their scopes. Buck and Toni raced back to Isabel. Both she and Lobo were looking through their eyepieces. Buck raised his binoculars, found the dead tree, and scanned to the bison skull and up the hill to the dark hole. Nothing was there.

"I missed it!" he said disappointedly. Lobo looked over at him.

"Jord only peeked out for a second and then ducked back in," he said, and stepped back from his scope. "Here, you look through my scope and let me use your binoculars. It won't be long before there's more activity."

Isabel stepped back, offering her scope to Toni, and as Buck and Toni looked through the scopes, Lobo and Isabel kept watch with the binoculars.

"Oh, wow!" Buck suddenly exclaimed. A big gray wolf sauntered out of a thick cluster of junipers thirty yards from the den. The wolf stretched and then trotted around, lifting his leg to urinate on several different bushes and rocks.

"That's Odin. He's marking his territory," Lobo said, keeping the binoculars to his eyes.

"Is he wearing a collar?" Toni asked.

"Yes," Lobo said. "It's a radio-tracking collar. We put them on two or three wolves from each pack so we can keep track of where the pack is."

The wolf wandered from bush to bush and then lay

down in the sun. Seconds later, two more wolves came out from the same cluster of junipers.

"Those are Geri and Freki," Lobo said.

"Which one is which?" Toni asked.

"Geri was the first one. Her legs are tanner than Freki's," Lobo said. "Freki's legs are almost white."

Geri wandered above the den, sniffing at clumps of sagebrush. Freki walked directly over to the den and stuck her head inside. Then she moved back and sat next to the leveled patch of dirt. It wasn't long before a black wolf poked its head out of the den. It looked around, surveying the territory, then climbed out. A white triangle was easily spotted on her black chest. She, too, had on a tracking collar. She trotted away, squatted to relieve herself, and then wandered over to where Odin had lain down in the sun.

"Is that Jord?" Buck asked.

"Yes," Lobo answered.

Jord sniffed Odin's nose, but instead of lying down, she lifted her head and stared across the open space toward the line of spotters.

"She's looking this way," Buck said. "Do you think she can see us?"

"Yes," Lobo said. "They have very keen vision, and really clue in on movement. They know we're here, but because they're protected in the park and have never been shot at, they're not concerned at this distance. Wolves outside the park would be more wary."

As he spoke, a black wolf pup suddenly tumbled out of the den. Immediately, a gray pup scrambled out over the black one's back, lost its footing, and did a somersault off the flattened area. The two-toned pup came out soon afterward, plopped down and scratched its ear with a hind foot. Freki trotted down the hill to the gray pup, picked it up by the scruff of its neck, and carried it back to the flat area. She dropped it in between the other two pups and then lay back down. Resting her head on her paws, she watched the pups like a vigilant babysitter as they frolicked and played.

"Oh, aren't they cute?" Toni said. Similar comments from the spotters could be heard going up and down the line.

"Are the pups males or females?" Buck asked, not

moving his eye from the scope.

"We don't know yet," Lobo answered. "It's hard to tell from this distance, and we generally don't interfere with the wolves except for collaring."

"How old are they?" Toni asked.

"About seven weeks," Lobo stated.

Buck and Toni took turns with Lobo and Isabel, switching back and forth between spotting scopes and binoculars. Odin, Jord, and Geri rested in the sun, but Freki kept guard, watching the pups as they played, tumbling over each other and climbing all over the older wolf.

"Shoop has gotten some fantastic footage," Dad said, coming back over to the others. "Did you see the two-toned pup chew on Freki's ear?"

"Yeah, it almost looked like it was playing tug-of-war with it," Buck answered, stepping aside to let his father look through Isabel's scope.

Toni was now looking through Lobo's scope. "Hey," she said in alarm. "Odin, Jord, and Geri are all leaving!"

Dad let Buck look back through the scope. The three

wolves had trotted away from the den, heading north and leaving the pups with Freki. Odin was in the lead, with Jord close behind. Geri was following a few feet back. Buck watched until the three disappeared behind a rise. Then he looked back at the den. Freki was standing now, holding the black pup by the neck. She went into the den with it, and the other two pups followed her in. All Buck could see now was a dark hole in the side of the distant hill.

"Show's over for today," Lobo said. "Freki will keep the pups in the den while the others go hunt. They could be gone for hours."

TAKE 8:

"TROTTING AT ITS AVERAGE PACE OF 8-10 MPH, A WOLF MAY TRAVEL MORE THAN FIFTY MILES IN SEARCH OF FOOD."

As soon as Freki took the pups in the den, the spotters immediately put up their scopes, and within minutes one vehicle after another was turning around and driving back toward the main road. Soon, only two vehicles remained—Isabel's and Lobo's.

"That was awesome! It was just like I was standing right in front of the den," Shoop said as he brought his equipment over to the SUV.

"I can't wait to see what you shot," Toni said.

"I can't wait to have lunch," Buck stated.

Dad looked at his watch. "Wow, we've watched those wolves for over two hours. It's almost eleven."

"Do we have to wait until noon?" Buck groaned. "I'll starve to death."

Dad laughed. "You won't starve, but I think we're all pretty hungry. We'll have an early lunch. Would you like to join us, Lobo? We have plenty of sandwiches."

"Thanks," Lobo answered, "but I've got to get back to the office."

"Where's that?" Buck said.

"In Mammoth," Lobo said as he put his scope in his truck. "Across the road from the Albright Visitor Center."

They said goodbye to Lobo, and soon the five of them were the only ones left on the hill overlooking Slough Creek.

"Up this road is a ranger station," Isabel said. "It's not currently manned, so we won't be able to go in, but it's got a great view of this whole valley and a picnic table. It would be a nice place to eat lunch."

"That sounds like a good idea," Dad said.

As they packed their equipment into the back of Isabel's

SUV, a small red car came down the road. A young woman in the passenger seat waved as they passed.

"I wonder if they're wolf spotters," Toni said to Buck.

Buck shrugged. "Beats me, but if they are, they're too late." He took one last look through the binoculars at the dark hole on the side of the hill. Still seeing no activity, he climbed into the ranger's vehicle.

It wasn't a long drive, but they slowed to view a small herd of bison, and the rutted dirt road also made driving slow.

"Man, my car is going to be a mess," Isabel complained as mud kept splattering all over her vehicle from numerous unavoidable puddles.

Finally the road ended in a long, sloping, puddle-strewn parking area. Down at the bottom, a black pickup with a camper shell was parked near a gate that blocked off another road. The red car, now muddy, was straight ahead, parked in front of an outhouse. The young woman who had waved at them was sitting on the edge of the car's open hatchback, changing from sneakers to hiking boots. A large backpack leaned against the side of the car, a sleeping bag strapped to the top. A young man lifted another pack from the back of the car and set it against the back bumper. Isabel pulled into a parking space uphill from the red car, a big puddle covering the two spaces between them.

"That's the ranger station," Isabel said, pointing to a rustic building down in the valley beyond the gate. "I don't have the keys to the gate, so we'll have to walk down to it, but I thought we might need a bathroom break first."

"If there's one thing I've learned while wandering around in the wilderness," Toni said, "is never turn down the chance to use a restroom. No telling where the next one will be!"

As Toni headed to the outhouse door marked WOMEN and Dad to the side marked MEN, Isabel walked around the mud puddle and over to the red car. Buck and Shoop stayed by the SUV. Buck put his binoculars to his eyes, looking at the pickup by the gate. Mud was splattered all over it, covering the license plate so thickly, Buck couldn't even tell what color the plate was.

"Hello," Isabel said to the young woman. "How far are

you going?"

"About seven miles, to Pebble Creek, and then back out tomorrow," the young woman answered. "We have time for only a short trip, but I hope we hear wolves howl."

"There's a good chance of that," Isabel said. "There are plenty around. And bears, too. Glad to see you have bear spray. Do you have backcountry permits?"

"Right there," the young man said, pointing to a tag tied to the backpack leaning against the bumper. Isabel walked over to the pack, but instead of looking at the tag, she turned to the man.

"I hope you're not thinking about flying that here," she said. Buck put the binoculars down to see Isabel glancing in the open hatchback door.

"No, we know they aren't allowed to be flown in the park," the man said. "Abby's in the drone competition in Gardiner Sunday afternoon."

The young woman stood up and put her sneakers in the back. Then the man reached up and shut the hatchback door.

"That's why we can't backpack longer," Abby added.

The man picked up the backpack and held it up while Abby put her arms in through the straps.

"I thought the competition was tomorrow," Buck said, walking over toward the backpackers.

"The junior division is," Abby said. "Sunday is for those over eighteen."

"You must be pretty good, being in a competition," Buck said as Toni came up beside him.

"I'm just a beginner," Abby said.

"Abby is just being modest," the man said. He picked up the other backpack and swung it onto his back. "She took a course in college last semester, and next semester she'll have another course on how to build her own drone."

"Cool," Buck said. "I'd like to learn to fly one."

"They'll have classes for beginners tomorrow. You ought to take one," the man said.

"That would be awesome, but I don't own a drone," Buck said.

"Not a problem. They'll have some for people to use," Abby said, tightening her pack's waist belt. The young couple said goodbye, and as Buck turned to watch them head toward the trail, he noticed that Shoop had his camera out. The red light was on, and he was following the backpackers as they left.

"Were you filming that whole thing?" Buck asked Shoop when the light went off.

"Yep," Shoop said. He returned the camera to its backpack and put his arms through the straps. "Thought it might be a bit of interest, showing a couple going off backpacking."

"Maybe we should try that," Buck said.

"No way," Shoop answered. "We have enough stuff to lug around without having to carry sleeping bags, tents, food, and everything else you'd need."

"We could use a backpack right now, though," Dad said as he started to pull out the cooler.

"We can carry lunch in my backpack," Toni offered.

"Thanks," Dad said. He loaded the pack and swung it to his back. Isabel took her scope case, Toni picked up the shotgun microphone's case, and Shoop put on his camera's backpack. Buck grabbed Isabel's binoculars, and they headed toward the gate, Buck and Toni in the lead.

"Can you make out the license plate number?" Buck asked Toni as they got closer to the pickup.

"No," Toni said, "but really, Buck. Not every black pickup is going to belong to the Deksters. There are tons of them."

"I guess," Buck said, but he wasn't convinced.

There was no fence attached to the gate, but several boulders had been placed on either side of the gateposts to keep motorists from driving around it. The five stepped off the road, walked between two of the boulders, and continued back onto the road on the other side. After about a quarter of a mile, the road divided. Isabel headed left.

"Where's that go?" Buck asked, looking the other way.

"Slough Creek Campground," Isabel answered, "but it doesn't open until June."

Soon they reached the ranger station. It sat at the head of the wide valley surrounded by steep hillsides. The sparkling waters of Slough Creek rushed a hundred yards in front of the rustic building's porch, and far in the distance, great purple mountains rose.

"This view is beautiful," Dad said.

"One of my favorite spots," Isabel said. She set her case on a picnic table that was near a flagpole. Buck set Isabel's binoculars near her case, then scanned the valley with his own.

"Look! Elk!" he called out. "About a half a mile down and on the other side of the creek. There must be at least fifty of them!"

Toni grabbed Isabel's binoculars. Shoop quickly pulled his camera out of his backpack and attached it to his tripod. Isabel did the same with her spotting scope.

"All cows and calves. One, way in back of the others, seems to be injured. And even farther down, you can see that bison herd we passed," Isabel said.

"Really?" Buck said.

"Here, take a look through this," Isabel said.

Buck handed Isabel his binoculars and looked through the scope. The elk were all bunched pretty close together, slowly ambling toward them as they grazed alongside the creek. Buck moved the scope, following the creek downstream until he saw the injured elk. It was a hundred yards away from the others but was moving slowly north toward the rest of the herd, limping as it walked. Buck moved the scope some more, looking for the bison, but stopped.

"Wolves!" he exclaimed.

TAKE 9:

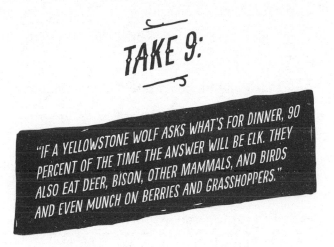

"IF A YELLOWSTONE WOLF ASKS WHAT'S FOR DINNER, 90 PERCENT OF THE TIME THE ANSWER WILL BE ELK. THEY ALSO EAT DEER, BISON, OTHER MAMMALS, AND BIRDS AND EVEN MUNCH ON BERRIES AND GRASSHOPPERS."

It was only seconds after Buck yelled "Wolves!" and Shoop was up on the picnic table with his camera screwed onto the tripod. Dad stepped up on the bench to look at the screen over Shoop's shoulder. Isabel put Buck's binoculars to her eyes.

"Where?" Toni said, still looking through Isabel's binoculars.

"Just inside the edge of that thick grove of aspen trees beyond the injured elk. I can see two of them. Looks like Jord and Geri."

"I can't find them," Toni said.

"Come over here," Dad said. "Shoop's got them spotted."

Toni handed the binoculars to Dad. Looking at the screen, she watched the two wolves—one black and the other two-toned—peer out of the woods. The injured elk had stepped into the creek and was taking a drink, apparently unaware that predators were watching it. Then the black wolf turned and disappeared.

"Look," Buck said. "Jord is sneaking off to the south."

"I lost track of her," Shoop said.

"She's in the woods," Buck said. "If you focus on the trees, you can see glimpses of her here and there between the tree trunks."

"Got her," Shoop said.

"And Geri is heading north now," Buck said. "I wonder where Odin is. Does anybody see him?"

"No, he might have separated from the others after they left the den," Isabel said. "But these two are setting up for the hunt. They'll probably go for the injured elk. Working as a team, they'll come at her from different directions."

As she spoke, Jord came out of the woods, trotting across the open expanse downstream of the elk. When she reached the water's edge, she slowly walked upstream toward her prey, keeping her head and shoulders low. The injured elk still stood in the creek, its head down, drinking.

"It doesn't look like the elk even knows the wolf is there," Buck said quietly.

"The wolf is downwind," Isabel said. "The elk wouldn't be able to smell it and isn't looking in the right direction."

As Isabel spoke, Jord charged toward the elk from the south. At the same time, Geri came rushing out of the woods in a full run at an angle from the northwest. The elk instantly jerked its head up and, in a flash, turned to escape. It ran downstream alongside the creek, limping with its injured leg, but the black wolf was in its path, only yards away. The elk veered into the creek, stumbling in the rushing water, and turned northward again.

"Geri's blocking it off," Buck called out as the two toned wolf splashed into a shallow, rippling section of the creek, stopping the elk's northern escape. The elk quickly turned again, moving into a deeper pool made where the creek curved against the six-foot-tall dirt wall of a cut bank, which blocked off any escape to the east. Geri stood her ground as Jord came up to the water's edge downstream of the elk. Neither wolf made any more advances, but from their positions, the two pack members stared at the elk, which now stood belly-deep in a pool of fast-moving water. Except for its head, which kept moving from side to side, keeping track of both wolves, the elk was motionless. But, all the while, it shrieked high-pitched sounds of distress that echoed up the valley.

"Why did the elk go in the water?" Buck asked. "Why didn't it just run the other way, toward the woods?"

"It went in the water as a defensive move," Isabel said. "Plus, it's injured and knows it can't outrun the wolves."

"Wow! Look at the other elk," Toni said. "They're running this way!"

Buck lifted his head from the spotting scope. The rest of the herd was now racing across the open grassland along the creek in a tight mass. In seconds, they were directly opposite the ranger station. Only the creek separated the film crew from the majestic creatures. The whole herd turned to the west and ran up a hill, and soon their white rumps quickly disappeared over a ridge.

Looking through the scope again, Buck returned to the wolves. The black one paced along the creek bank, every now and then making threatening lunges, keeping the elk moving back and forth in the water but giving it no room to escape from the creek. The two-toned wolf stood perfectly still in ankle-deep water, watching.

"Why aren't they attacking?" Buck asked.

"It's harder for wolves to kill their prey while swimming than by chasing them down on land," Isabel said. "They're wearing the elk down, tiring it out. Since there's only two of them, it will make it easier for them to take the elk down if it's tired out."

For several minutes the wolves patrolled their stations, not seeming to be in any hurry. Geri took a drink, Jord sat down and scratched herself with a hind leg, but neither took their eyes off their prey. The elk became more and more frantic, turning this way and that and still making the shrill sounds.

Geri made the first move. With a giant leap, she sprang into the deep water, swimming toward the elk. With water flying, the elk crashed out onto the shore and started running toward the woods, but Jord was right behind, grabbing at its back legs with an opened mouth. The elk kicked back and spun around, trying to butt the wolf with its head, but the wolf quickly darted out of reach, racing around and trying to snare a back leg again. Over and over, the elk bucked and kicked, circled and rammed, but now Geri had reached them. She entered the fight, also trying to bite a hind leg.

"Elk aren't totally defenseless," Isabel said. "They can severely injure or even kill a wolf with a kick. But the wolves know if they can grab hold of a hind leg, the elk can't kick and can't run."

"Do you think that's why the elk was injured in the first place?" Toni asked. "From a wolf bite?"

"Could be," Isabel said. "But probably it broke its leg some other way, and it didn't mend well."

"Look! Geri's got hold of its leg!" Buck said. "And Jord's coming around to its front!"

Now, with Geri biting down tight and pulling backward on the injured hind leg and Jord lunging at the elk's neck, the elk could no longer keep fighting by twisting and kicking. The black wolf sank its sharp teeth into the elk's neck, and it wasn't long before the elk went down.

"I feel bad for the elk," Toni said as the wolves started to feed.

"A predator taking down its prey can be hard to watch," Isabel said, "but it's all part of nature. Each animal has a role in the scheme of things."

They watched the wolves tear into the fallen elk, pulling off pieces of meat. As they ate, some coyotes trotted out from the woods. They didn't approach the wolves but sat down several yards away, watching. Five ravens flew over the roof of the ranger's station, cawing to one another as they flapped over the valley toward the kill. Landing in a branch of a dead tree, they, too, watched the wolves eat.

Soon a pair of magpies joined the onlookers, landing on the ground near the wolves. One of the coyotes got up and trotted closer to the elk, but Geri growled and made a short lunge at it. The coyote turned and ran back to the others, tail between its legs. But as Geri lunged, one of the magpies took the opportunity to jump over to the carcass and quickly nip off a bite. In a rustling of black and white feathers, it flew a few feet, landing on the ground to enjoy its meal as Geri returned to hers.

"One elk kill obviously doesn't just feed wolves," Toni said.

"You're right," Isabel agreed. "It feeds a lot of other animals as well. When the wolves have had their fill and leave, the coyotes will eat."

"Won't the wolves drag the carcass back to the den?" Buck asked.

"No, when they return to the den, Freki and Odin will probably come down to feed," Isabel answered. "They'll scare the coyotes off the kill, but if a bear gets a whiff, the wolves won't even have a chance."

"What about the pups?" Toni asked. "Will Freki and Odin bring them with them?"

"No," Isabel said. "Jord will feed the pups some regurgitated elk meat."

"Re-what?" Buck asked.

"Regurgitated," Isabel said. "She'll bring up some of the swallowed food for the pups to eat."

"You mean like vomiting?" Toni said. "That's disgusting."

"It's kind of like vomiting, except the meat won't have had time to be digested," Isabel explained. "But it has been chewed up, so it's easier for the pups to eat at their young age. Vomiting is usually because you're sick. Regurgitation is done on purpose. Lots of animals regurgitate food for their young."

"All this talk about food is making me hungry," Buck said, turning to his dad. "When's lunch?"

"Not sure I can stomach any lunch now," Shoop said, holding his belly. "I've filmed enough. I think I'm going to go sit down for a minute." Shoop turned off the camera and walked over to the porch. He sat down on the step and then he put his head between his knees.

Toni turned to Isabel. "My dad has a weak stomach. It doesn't take much to get it upset."

"Yeah," Dad said. "We were on a shoot in the Gulf of Mexico once, and all someone had to do was hold out a greasy, chicken-fried steak sandwich, asking Shoop if he wanted a bite. Instantly, Shoop was at the rails of the boat, seasick."

"It wasn't funny," Shoop said without raising his head. "And if I think too much about it right now, I might be sick again."

"Sorry. I shouldn't have brought it up," Dad said to Shoop, but Buck started chuckling.

"What's so funny?" Toni said.

"Dad said he shouldn't have brought it up," Buck said. "But Dad didn't bring it up—it's Shoop who's about to regurgitate!"

"Enough, Buck!" Dad said. "Go take Shoop a bottle of water, and apologize."

Buck grabbed a bottle from Toni's backpack. "Sorry," he said as he handed the water to Shoop.

"That's okay, dude," Shoop said, and when he lifted his head, he had a little grin on his face. "I thought your dad's choice of words was a bit comical too."

"Do you want a sandwich?" Buck asked seriously.

"No, I think I'll pass on that for the moment," Shoop said.

TAKE 10:

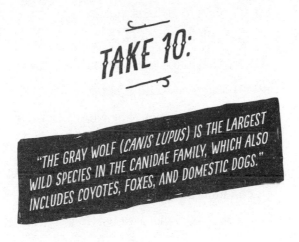

"THE GRAY WOLF (*CANIS LUPUS*) IS THE LARGEST WILD SPECIES IN THE CANIDAE FAMILY, WHICH ALSO INCLUDES COYOTES, FOXES, AND DOMESTIC DOGS."

As Shoop sat on the porch, the others ate their lunch, keeping their eyes on the wolves, which also ate in the distance. Soon they all had finished, including the two wolves, which trotted side by side down the middle of the valley in the direction of the den. The coyotes settled in on a meal as the ravens and magpies hopped between and around them, snatching a bite here and there.

Packing up their equipment and trash, the film crew headed back until they reached where the road divided.

"Is the campground far?" Shoop asked Isabel. "I'd like

to film it, if it's okay to go in there."

"Sure," Isabel said. "It's not far."

Buck glanced back toward the parking area as they turned the opposite way. The pickup was still there. He put the binoculars to his eyes. The front license plate was also too muddy to read. Buck dropped the binoculars and jogged to catch up with the others. Just as he caught up, Isabel stopped and looked at the road.

"Someone else has walked down here recently," she said.

"Yep," Buck said, seeing several boot tracks in the gravely dirt. He kept on walking.

"No, look again," Isabel said.

"A grizzly track!" Toni said, stopping beside the ranger. "We saw some in Alaska, too! Do you think a bear is going to scare the coyotes off the elk kill?"

"It's always a possibility," Isabel said. "These tracks are a few days old, but you always want to pay attention out here."

Buck hurried back and looked at the huge print. It was not as clear as one he and Toni had seen in the mud on an Alaskan riverbed, but he could definitely make out the rounded pad and the pointed claw marks near each toe impression.

"Cool," he said. "That's amazing that you spotted it!" He pulled his camera from his pocket and snapped a picture. Then, squatting down, he placed his hand next to the track and snapped another picture before they resumed walking.

The campground was situated in a grove of spruce trees that lined the east side of Slough Creek. Picnic tables, fire rings, and short parking areas for each campsite were scattered alongside the creek. In shady spots, patches of snow were still on the ground, and everywhere, there was bison dung.

"Look!" Buck called out. A fox was nosing around in one of the fire rings, but as soon as Buck spoke, it grabbed something from inside the ring and ran off, disappearing into the trees upstream. "Did you see that? It grabbed a chunk of bread."

Buck jogged over to the ring. Sitting on top of old, soggy ashes was a wadded-up wrapper from a fast-food sandwich and a scattering of onion slices.

"I guess whoever ate this didn't like onions," Toni said, coming up beside him.

"Obviously, the fox didn't like onions either," Buck said. "But whoever it was, he ate here today. Those onions are fresh."

Shoop had pulled out his camera and was panning the empty campground.

"Did you get the fox?" Toni asked him.

"No, missed him. But I need some shots for filler," Shoop said. "Buck, go do something. Anything that comes to mind."

Buck walked over to the creek's edge, picked up a stone, and flicked it out over the water. It made three skips across the surface. Buck picked up another. This one skipped five long skips, then ended with several short little skips before landing on the bank on the other side.

"Okay," Shoop said. "Do something else."

Buck looked around. A tree had fallen across a shallow section of the creek, its big root ball on the near bank. Buck stepped up on the wide end of the trunk and started walking. He purposely wobbled back and forth, his arms raised to either side like he was trying to keep his balance.

"Stop fooling around. If you fall in and get wet," Dad warned, "I don't want to hear any complaining."

"I won't fall," Buck said. As the tree trunk narrowed, Buck slowed down and concentrated more, finally jumping onto the far bank. He turned around and started back, but once the trunk got wider, Buck showed off again, leaping his way back.

"Wow," Toni said. "You looked like you could be on a gymnastics team."

"I took classes when I lived with my grandparents," Buck answered.

"I didn't know that," Dad said.

"It was all Grandma's idea," Buck said. "She thought I needed something to keep me busy."

Isabel chuckled. "I can imagine."

"Okay," Shoop said. "Just one more thing. Go stand up on one of the picnic tables and look through your binoculars. Maybe at that far hill over there, like you see something of interest."

Buck jumped up on the nearest table and lifted his binoculars. Across the creek was a treeless meadow, and beyond it, a tall steep hill rose sharply with some rock outcroppings near the top. Buck focused in on the rocks, then scanned the hillside to the south.

"Holy cow!" he called out. "There *is* something over there. It looks like Odin!"

Toni was instantly on the table beside Buck, with Isabel's binoculars to her eyes. Isabel started unzipping the spotting scope case, and Shoop jumped onto another table and quickly had his camera set up on his tripod. Dad stepped up on the bench behind Shoop.

"I see him," Toni said. "It looks like he's taking a nap."

Isabel stepped up beside Buck and Toni, and the two scooted closer together to give her room to set her tripod with the scope on the table.

"Where?" Isabel asked.

"Start at the rock outcropping," Buck said, "and then look to the south, several hundred yards. He's right out in the open, in the sun."

"I found him, but something's not right!" she blurted

out with alarm.

"What do you mean?" Buck said.

"The way he's lying—it doesn't look right," Isabel said, still looking through the eyepiece. "Something's wrong with him, I'm certain. He looks like he's unconscious. Can you tell if he's breathing, Shoop?"

"I've got him zoomed in as close as I can," Shoop said, "and I don't see any movement. If he's breathing, it's really shallow."

Isabel jumped down from the table.

"I'm going over there, Dan. I need to get closer to tell if he's okay. Will you come with me?" Isabel asked. "It'd be safer with more than one person."

"I'll go!" Buck said instantly, leaping from the table.

"Me too!" Toni said, jumping down beside Buck.

"No," Isabel, Dad, and Shoop all said at the same time. Then Dad turned to Isabel.

"Of course I'll go with you. I wouldn't let you go by yourself! Should Shoop come too?"

Shoop looked at Dad like the idea was totally unthinkable, but he said, "I'll come if you need me to."

"I think just Dan and I will be enough," Isabel said.

Buck looked at his father. "If I went, Shoop could film me."

"No," Dad said. "And that's final. Shoop will find some way of making it look like you're there."

"What if Odin isn't unconscious?" Toni asked. "What if he wakes up when you're near him?"

"If he does, he'll probably just run the other way. But if a wolf stands its ground, you keep eye contact with it, make yourself look bigger, and yell and wave your arms as you slowly back away," Isabel said. "And if he comes at us, bear spray works on wolves, too." She patted the holstered canister attached to her belt. Then she pulled the radio off the other side of her belt.

"Buck, will you go find a long stick for me? About as long as you are tall," Isabel said.

"Sure," Buck said. As he looked around on the ground, he heard the radio make some crackling, static sounds.

"Yellowstone Dispatch, over," a scratchy voice came over the radio.

"This is Ranger Hodges," Isabel said into the radio.

"Badge number six-eleven-seventy-seven. Please connect me with Chuck Donaldson, number one-zero-five-seventeen. Over."

"One moment, please. Over."

Buck found a long, slender stick just as Lobo's voice came over the radio.

"What's up, Isabel? Over."

"We've got a situation. Odin is down. I don't know if he's just unconscious . . ." Isabel paused and glanced over at Buck and Toni like she was hesitant to say more, but then she continued. "Or dead. Over."

Buck's mouth dropped open, and he quickly looked at Toni. She seemed just as stunned as he was. Buck leaned the stick against the table, then he jumped back up and looked through the scope, trying to see if he could detect any rise or fall in the wolf's side.

"Do you think he's dead?" Toni whispered as she climbed up beside him.

Buck shrugged. "I don't know."

"Where is he? Over," Lobo asked.

"About three-quarters of a mile south of Slough Creek

Campground. West of the creek up on the hillside. We spotted him from the campground. Over," Isabel answered.

"Can you tell if he's breathing? Over," Lobo said.

"No, he's too far away," Isabel said. "Dan and I are going up there to get a closer look. Over."

"I'll contact a chopper and have them on standby," Lobo said. "Keep me posted. Over."

"Okay," Isabel stated. "Over."

"And, Isabel," Lobo said, "be careful. Over."

"I will," she replied. "Over and out."

Isabel put the radio back on her belt and picked up the stick. Hurrying over to the fallen tree, she stepped up on its trunk and started across Slough Creek. As soon as she reached the other side, Dad went across, and soon they were both heading up the hill. Shoop kept filming as Buck and Toni took turns with the scope and binoculars, trying to detect any signs of life in the gray wolf lying on the hillside.

It took about twenty minutes for Isabel and Dad to climb the steep hill. It was easy to see that they were both breathing hard as they finally reached the area with the rock outcroppings and stopped. The wolf never moved. Isabel took the bear spray from its holster, and the two cautiously advanced until they were only about twenty yards away. They stopped again. Isabel and Dad talked for a second, and then Dad took the canister from Isabel. With Dad aiming the spray canister toward the wolf, they slowly approached the animal, stopping a few feet in front of it. Dad stayed where he was, the bear spray aimed as Isabel took a step forward. She gently poked the animal in its side with the stick.

Buck saw no movement. His throat tightened and his muscles tensed as he watched Isabel step closer and kneel beside the wolf. She put one hand on the wolf's side and the other under its neck and held them there a few seconds. Then, standing back up, Isabel looked over at Dad, said something, and shook her head. Dad walked over to Isabel's side, handed her the canister of bear spray, and the two stood there, looking down at the lifeless wolf.

"Oh no," Buck said, tears streaming down his face. Toni had tears, too. Shoop left the camera running and came over to the other table, wiping his eyes with the back of his sleeve.

"Come on down," he said quietly, and when the two kids climbed off the table, the three of them stood embracing one another.

TAKE 11:

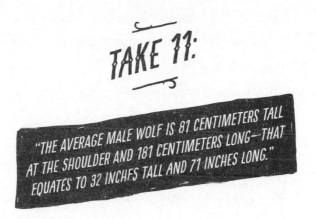

"THE AVERAGE MALE WOLF IS 81 CENTIMETERS TALL AT THE SHOULDER AND 181 CENTIMETERS LONG—THAT EQUATES TO 32 INCHES TALL AND 71 INCHES LONG."

"I can't believe it," Buck said as the three stepped apart. "He looked so healthy this morning at the den."

Toni sniffled and wiped her eyes. "What do you think happened? Do you think an elk kicked him?"

"He might have gotten into a fight with a wolf from another pack," Buck said. "Lobo told me they do that."

Buck raised his binoculars and looked up the hill again. Isabel was talking into the radio, but Dad was motioning to them.

"Dad's telling us to come up," he said, and started

running toward the fallen tree.

"Buck, we can't leave the equipment here," Shoop said. "Come back and help."

Soon they had it all packed away again, and everyone was carrying something.

"Be careful," Shoop said as Buck stepped up on the tree. "Don't drop anything in the creek."

"I won't," Buck said, and hurried across. Toni quickly followed him, but Shoop stepped up on the wide part of the trunk just in front of the root ball and stopped.

"You can do it, Shoop," Toni encouraged. "And if you fall off, you'll be okay. The water's only about knee-deep."

"The equipment is making me off balance," Shoop offered as an excuse. Buck set the case containing Isabel's scope on the ground and hopped back up onto the tree trunk.

"You're bouncing it," Shoop said, and jumped back onto the ground.

"I'm not," Buck said. He quickly spanned the creek, jumped down, and ran over to where he had found a stick for Isabel. He came back with an even longer stick.

"Here," he said, handing it to Shoop. "I'll take the equipment, and you can use this. It should reach all the way to the bottom."

"Do you think the far end will hold me?" Shoop said.

"Sure," Buck said as he put on Shoop's camera backpack and looped the tripod case strap over his shoulder. "It held Dad and Isabel. You go first."

"They probably weakened it," Shoop muttered under his breath as he stepped up on the trunk again. He slowly started across, poking the makeshift walking stick into the rocky creek bed as he went. Buck was right behind him, but Shoop slowed down even more as the trunk narrowed.

"Don't stop," Buck said. "That's when you lose your balance."

Shoop finally got to the other side.

"You're ready for the Olympics now, Shoop," Toni teased him.

"I'd be okay if there wasn't water flowing underneath," Shoop said. "The movement makes me dizzy."

"Leave the stick here," Buck suggested. "You'll want it

when we come back."

Shoop dropped the stick on the bank and took his equipment from Buck. Buck picked up Isabel's case, and the three of them started up the hill. They were almost to the rock outcroppings when they heard the sound of a helicopter coming up the valley. Isabel waved her arms above her head.

The chopper hovered far enough away from where Isabel and Dad stood that they were not blasted by the winds that beat the grasses below it. But the chopper remained about forty feet in the air, as close to the ground as possible without the rotors hitting the sides of the steeply slanted hillside. The back door slid open. Lobo was inside. With a rope, he quickly lowered a large plastic box to the ground. Then the helicopter lifted up and flew directly over Buck, Toni, and Shoop. Turning, Buck watched it land in a clearing just beyond the campground. As the three hurried on, Dad walked over, got the box, and placed it near the wolf.

"What do you think happened?" Buck asked as they reached Isabel and Dad. They were standing several feet from the wolf.

"I don't know. There's not a mark on him," Isabel said sadly. She let out a long sigh. "He was such a magnificent creature."

Buck started for the wolf, but Isabel stopped him. "Stay back here with us," she said. "Lobo needs to see him just as we found him."

As Buck returned to Isabel's side, he could see Lobo. He had crossed the river and was more than halfway up to the rocks, almost jogging.

"Shoop," Isabel said. "This may seem inappropriate, but could you film this? If we do catch whoever is killing animals, we may be able to use your recordings to help convict him."

"Whatever I can do to help," Shoop said.

When Lobo finally reached them, he walked straight over to the box and pulled out a pair of rubber gloves. Then he knelt by the wolf and examined the animal. He rubbed his hands all up and down the wolf's side, around its neck, and under its chin. Turning it over, he inspected the other side. The wolf's outer guard hairs were coarse, but underneath, the fur was thick, fluffy, and soft-looking.

"This makes me so angry," he said, his face grim. "I'm betting he was poisoned. The autopsy on the coyotes came back positive for cyanide, and it doesn't look as if this wolf has had any physical trauma."

"What's cyanide?" Buck asked.

"A deadly poison," Lobo answered. "Even if we had gotten to him immediately, there wouldn't have been much we could do except put him out of his misery."

"Is it painful?" Toni asked.

"It causes severe abdominal pains, along with a bunch of other symptoms," Lobo said. "Did you find any vomit up here?"

"Yes," Dad said. "I noticed some when I went over to get the box."

"Show me where. I'll send it to the lab," Lobo said, taking a plastic container and spoon from the box. "And keep your eyes open for anything else unusual."

He and Dad walked away, both keeping their eyes to the ground. As Lobo knelt to gather the sample, Dad scoured the area around it. When they returned, Lobo rummaged around in the box and brought out a spiral notebook and pen, a measuring tape, a small plastic box, and several pairs of rubber gloves.

"I'm going to take some measurements," Lobo stated, and looked at Buck. "Do you and Toni want to help me?"

"Sure," Buck answered.

Toni took off her earphones and handed them and the shotgun mic to Dad.

Giving gloves to both kids, Lobo knelt down near Odin's head. Buck and Toni knelt down on the other side. Lobo unbuckled Odin's tracking collar and set it aside. Then he opened the small box. In it were syringes and vials. He filled three vials with the wolf's blood, labeled them, and put them back in the small box, along with the syringe. Finally he handed Buck the measuring tape and Toni the notebook and pen.

"You'll be my assistant, Buck," Lobo said. "And, Toni, you'll record the data."

Toni flipped open the notebook and clicked the end of the pen. Lobo opened the wolf's mouth and pulled up its lip, exposing the sharp, slightly curved teeth.

"Teeth—all forty-two in good shape," Lobo said. He looked up at Toni to make sure she was writing it down. "Buck, how long is his canine tooth?"

"The fanglike one?" Buck asked.

"Yes," Lobo said. Buck pulled the measuring tape out and laid it along the longest tooth in the wolf's mouth.

"Ummm," he said, looking up at Lobo with a puzzled expression. "This doesn't look right. It's more than two, but these aren't inches, are they?"

"It's a metric tape measure," Lobo explained. "The numbers indicate how many centimeters, and the little lines in between are millimeters. There are ten millimeters to a centimeter."

"Why don't you use a regular tape measure?" Buck asked.

"In science, we usually use metric measurements," Lobo said. "Everything is based on units of ten, which are a lot easier to add up than units of twelve."

"Oh," Buck said, and read off the measurement. "It's two centimeters and four millimeters."

"We also use decimals," Lobo said. "So we would

say two point four centimeters. The point four means four-tenths of a centimeter, which is the same as four millimeters."

Lobo looked over at the notebook as Toni wrote LEFT CANINE—*2.4 CM*.

"Perfect," Lobo told her.

Lobo had Buck measure the width and length of one front paw, the longest claw, the wolf's height from shoulder to foot, and its length from its nose to the tip of its tail.

"Okay, time to weigh him," Lobo said. He reached into his box and pulled out a metal bar with a hook hanging from it and some neatly folded nylon material. Lobo shook open the material. Four straps, each sewn onto a corner, had been folded up inside. Each strap had a metal ring on the end.

"That thing with the hook is a scale," Lobo said as he laid the material beside the wolf. "We'll put the wolf in this harness and lift him with the scale to see how much he weighs. Buck, you grab around his hind end, and I'll grab around his front."

"Man, he's heavy," Buck said as they picked up the wolf and set him back down on the harness.

"He was one of the bigger wolves in the park," Lobo said. He gathered up the straps and slid the metal rings onto the hook at the bottom of the scale.

"Okay, I'm going to need your help, Dan," Lobo said, and then he turned to Buck. "We're going to hold this bar and lift the wolf. Do you see that little screen in the round part between the bar and the hook?"

"Yes," Buck said. "It will show a digital readout of his weight, won't it?"

"Yes, and it will be in kilograms," Lobo said. "It will take a second to register, but read it as soon as it has a steady display. As you say, this guy's heavy."

With Dad gripping one end of the bar and Lobo the other, they lifted the wolf until it was swinging in its harness. Buck looked at the screen. Numbers kept changing, but then came to a stop.

"Fifty-three point six kilograms," Buck quickly said.

"I knew he was a big one," Isabel said as Dad and Lobo lowered the wolf back to the ground. "Average males are about forty-five to fifty kilograms."

"How many kilograms are in a pound?" Buck asked Lobo, but Toni answered instead.

"One kilogram is about two point two pounds," she said. "So, if you do the math . . ." Toni paused and quickly figured the math problem on the notebook. "One hundred and seventeen point nine pounds."

When Toni looked up, everyone was staring at her. "We had metric problems for homework last night," Toni stated.

Toni gave Buck a small, almost laughing smile, and he knew that if Shoop weren't filming, she would have said he obviously hadn't done his homework.

"Wow! Odin weighs a lot more than I weigh!" Buck said, choosing to ignore Toni's smug smile.

"I'm going to wish I was carrying *you* down to the helicopter instead of that wolf!" Lobo said.

"Why doesn't the helicopter fly up here and get him?" Buck said, surprised at Lobo's response.

"No place to land safely," Lobo answered. "Help me again, will you, Buck?"

They lifted the wolf off the harness, and Lobo started folding up the material again.

"I just can't figure it out. We've got to be missing something up here," he said. "Let's look around this whole area again—especially over where I got the vomit sample. Look for anything unusual. Maybe a dart with a needle and syringe, or . . ."

Lobo's voice trailed off. It was obvious that he didn't know what they should actually be looking for. They all spread out, walking away from the wolf, except Shoop. Shoop walked over to the animal lying lifeless on its side.

"Thanks for letting me film you, buddy," Shoop said quietly, squatting beside the wolf. "I'm sorry this had to happen to you. You were so beautiful this morning. So strong and proud."

"Shoop's got a real soft spot for dogs," Toni said quietly to Isabel as they walked, their eyes focused on the ground. "I think he's got one for wolves now, too."

Shoop stood up and, wandering away from where the others were, pulled a tissue from a pocket and blew his nose.

Lobo finally said, "Okay, that's enough. Let's get going."

As they turned around, Buck stepped on something, crushing it with his foot. He immediately stopped and, kneeling down, looked where his foot had landed.

"Did you find something?" Lobo asked.

"I don't know. It felt like I stepped on something," Buck said, separating the grasses with his gloved hands. "I did! It's all crushed, but it looks like it might have been a piece of dog food."

Lobo instantly dropped to his knees. "Don't touch it," he said. "I'll take it back to the lab. Toni, will you go get a baggie out of my box? They're on the left."

"Sure," Toni said, and raced to the box.

"There's a little brush in there," Lobo called out to her. "Bring it, too, please."

Soon Toni returned. Buck kept the grasses pulled aside as Lobo swept the crumbs into the baggie and zipped it shut.

"That was lucky," he said to Buck. "I'm certain it has something to do with Odin's death. Let's look to see if there is any more kibble around here."

Except for Shoop, who had started filming again the minute Buck said he had stepped on something, they all dropped to their knees, carefully searching through the grasses in the surrounding area. Noticing a speck of dust on his lens, Shoop turned off the camera and pulled a lens cloth from his pocket.

"Oops," he said.

Buck looked up and saw Shoop lean over, pick something up, and put it in his pocket.

"What was that?" Buck called out. "Did you find something?"

"No," Shoop said. "Just a tissue. It must have dropped out of my pocket."

"Oh," Buck said disappointedly, and went back to searching through the grass. Finally, after finding nothing, they all got to their feet and headed back to the wolf.

Lobo took the gloves from Buck and Toni and packed everything back into his box. Shoop and Dad helped drape the wolf's limp body over Lobo's shoulders. The others picked up various pieces of equipment, and they started down toward the campground.

"We thought the two coyotes might have gotten into one of the maintenance sheds and eaten some pesticides or weed killer," Lobo said. "The coyotes were found pretty close to Roosevelt Lodge."

"We passed that coming here this morning," Toni stated. "Just before we saw some Bighorn sheep."

"Coyotes aren't as leery of civilization, and being close to people doesn't bother them," Lobo said. "Some even live in cities. But wolves usually stay away from where people are, and this wolf certainly wasn't near any maintenance shed."

"How do you think the kibble got up there?" Buck asked.

"I don't know," Lobo said. "And first we have to determine if it even is kibble. It was pretty crushed, so we are just assuming it was dog food."

"Sorry," Buck said, "I didn't mean to step on it."

"No," Lobo said. "If you hadn't stepped on it, we would be lacking this one little piece of evidence. It may be the most important piece we have. But we'll have to test it to see exactly what it is and if it contains cyanide or some other kind of poison."

"I guess it could be just a piece of a granola bar or something that a hiker dropped, couldn't it?" Buck said.

"Exactly," Lobo said. "In science you have to thoroughly investigate all possibilities and not jump to conclusions."

"I'm worried," Shoop said. "What's going to happen to the other wolves and the pups without the alpha male?"

"Several things could happen," Lobo stated. "The pack could assimilate in with another pack. Or a lone wolf may come in to take over the alpha male's place. It will be more difficult for them for a while, since it's such a small pack, but they'll be fine."

"We already saw that Jord and Geri were able to bring down an elk," Buck told Lobo. "We watched it from the ranger station down there."

"Awesome," Lobo said. "Not many people get to witness that!"

They reached the creek. Lobo tromped through the water to the other side. Shoop watched the others cross on the log, but when it was his turn, he hesitated. Then, shaking his head, he stepped into the cold water and waded across. Then they all walked through the campground to where the helicopter and pilot were waiting.

As the rotors started spinning, Dad put Lobo's box in the back of the chopper. They all said their final goodbyes to Odin, giving him one last pet. Lobo laid the great gray wolf in back next to the box, but before he climbed in the chopper, he turned to the others.

"Do me a favor, will you?" Lobo yelled over the roar of the rotors. "Don't mention this to anyone. I don't want whoever killed Odin to know we discovered it. I want to catch this killer!"

TAKE 12:

"WOLVES HAVE VERY GOOD EYESIGHT AND EXCELLENT NIGHT VISION, BUT THEY CAN'T SEE REDS AND GREENS. TO THEM, THOSE COLORS LOOK LIKE SHADES OF YELLOW AND BLUE."

It was a quiet ride back to the campground, everyone deep in their own thoughts. At one point the SUV slowed to a creep in a long line of cars.

"Bison jam," Isabel stated. "Yellowstone's version of a traffic jam."

But even as they inched through a large herd that was walking right down the middle of the road, the sight of bison within arm's reach through the safety of the vehicle's rolled-up windows raised their spirits only for the moment.

When Isabel dropped them off at their campsite, she asked, "Is there anything else I can help you with?"

"No, but thanks for everything," Dad said. "It's been great getting to know you."

"It's too bad it had to end on such a sad note," Shoop added. "But keep us posted on what you find out about Odin."

"I will," Isabel promised. "When are you leaving?"

"Tuesday," Dad said. "It will take us at least a couple of days to edit what we have, and we may need to reshoot some scenes."

Isabel turned to Buck and Toni and gave them each a big hug. "You two are just super," she said. "Keep in touch with me, okay? And I'll make sure to watch your show."

As soon as Isabel drove away, Dad and Shoop took all the equipment into the Green Beast. Buck and Toni sat down outside at the picnic table.

"What do you want to do?" Toni asked. "It's only four o'clock."

"I don't know," Buck said. "You still owe me an ice

cream cone. Maybe we could take the trail to Mammoth. I'll go ask Dad."

Buck had barely gotten to his feet when Philo drove up.

"I was up on the top tier but rushed down here when I saw you pull in," he said, walking over to Buck and Toni. "I thought you might want to know—the coyotes were poisoned."

"We know," Buck said. "Isabel told us." It was all he could do to keep from blurting out about Odin.

"I was also worried about you guys," Philo said. "I heard a call go through to dispatch from Isabel, but everything after that was encrypted."

"What's that mean?" Buck asked.

"It's a way of blocking radio transmissions so only certain people can listen," Philo explained. "The rangers use that if messages contain sensitive information that they don't want the general public to hear."

"What did you hear?" Toni asked, glancing at Buck.

"Just that Isabel was contacting Lobo," Philo said. "Then it went dead."

"Oh," Buck said. "It was probably about the elk kill.

Lobo didn't get to see that."

Then the two told Philo about their day, ending with watching Jord and Geri taking down the injured elk.

"Well, you had a more eventful day than I did," Philo said. "The only thing that happened in the campground was a camper had a flat tire."

"You were going to talk with Jason Dekster this morning about that drone we saw," Buck said. "What did he say?"

"I didn't have a chance this morning," Philo said. "They left soon after you did. But I just now came from up there. I told them we'd had a report of a drone being flown in the campground. The boy didn't say anything, but the father just said, 'We know the rules.' I thought his tone was a little gruff."

"Well, maybe he'll think that you're onto him," Buck said, "and that will keep him from flying it here again."

"*If* it was him," Toni once again insisted. "Remember what Lobo said, not to jump to conclusions."

"She's right," Philo agreed. "But if he was the one, you might be right too, Buck. Maybe that will scare him from flying in the park again. Well, I have to mosey along. Glad you had an exciting day."

As Philo got into his golf cart and drove away, the Kolsons' RV slowly drove down the campground road. It pulled to a stop beside the campsite driveway.

"Did you see any wolves?" Kayla called out through the opened window. "We saw a grizzly!"

"Hop out," Toni said. "We'll tell you all about it."

The RV door opened, and Kayla and Kale jumped out. As the RV started driving away, Dad and Shoop came out of the camper.

"Can we show Kayla and Kale what we filmed today?" Toni asked Shoop.

"I saw them out here," Shoop said, "and figured you'd want to. It's all downloaded onto a thumb drive on your desk."

"Just remember what Lobo requested," Dad said quietly to Buck.

"We will," Buck said.

Inside, Toni brought the video up on her computer. She fast-forwarded past what Shoop had filmed at the meadow but showed them the bighorn sheep, before fast-forwarding again to the wolf den.

They watched the big gray wolf stroll out of the junipers and lay in the sun.

"That's Odin," Toni said. She quickly glanced over at Buck, a sad look on her face. Buck nodded his understanding as Kayla excitedly exclaimed how beautiful the big gray wolf was. As the video continued, Buck and Toni identified the different wolves—Geri and Freki as they came out into the open, and Jord, as she climbed out of the den.

"Oh, how cute!" Kayla said when the pups tumbled out of the den and played.

"You've got to see what's next," Buck said after the pups went back in the den with Freki. He reached across and fast-forwarded past the backpackers to the injured elk, limping into the creek for a drink.

"Oh, wow!" Kayla said as Jord came stalking up behind the unsuspecting elk. Kale hadn't said a word, but his eyes were glued to the computer screen. When Jord bounded toward the elk and Geri came charging toward it from the woods, Kale called out.

"GERUMAC!"

"The wolf isn't named Gerumac," his sister said. "It's named Geri."

"No, not the wolf, a GERUMAC. It's the acronym for a super drone," Kale said. He reached out and paused the video.

"Kale! What are you doing?" Kayla said.

The image froze in place. The black wolf stood on shore parallel to the elk, which was belly-deep in the middle of the creek. The two-toned wolf was in front of the elk, in ankle-deep water. But Kale pointed to a red speck just barely visible above the woods in the background. Around it, there seemed to be a grayish halo.

"That's a GERUMAC," he said. "They're awesome! Want to see one?"

Without waiting for a response, Kale reached over and put the video into the menu bar at the bottom of the computer screen. Then he opened up an Internet browser and started typing. Soon, across the screen in large capital letters was the word *GERUMAC*. Centered under the acronym was *GPS ENHANCED REMOTE*

UNMANNED AIRCRAFT. Kale scrolled down until the image of a large charcoal-colored quadcopter filled the screen. Four black blades were attached to the frame above the main body of the drone. There were two landing skids on either side of the main body. A bright red clawlike thing was attached under a camera that hung from underneath.

"There it is—the GERUMAC," Kale said excitedly. "One of the most powerful quadcopters on the market. It's got one of the best cameras, and with GPS, you don't have to keep it in sight to fly it. You just follow it on your phone. With two high-capacity batteries, you can fly almost an hour, and it can go over a five-mile radius. It even has a special case with shoulder straps for carrying it, like a backpack."

"Wow! It's really big," Buck said, thinking at the same time that he'd never heard Kale talk so much.

"Probably why we were able to see it in the video," Toni said.

"It weighs over seven kilograms," Kale said, "and can hold a kilogram of payload."

"What do you mean by payload?" Buck said.

"Cargo," Kale said. "It can carry and drop things. Like a pizza or a package. That red claw can grip a box, and it has a remote cargo release—just push a button; its claw opens and its cargo drops."

"So that's the super drone you've been talking about," Kayla said. "He keeps telling our parents that he could pay for one with pizza delivery tips."

"How much is a GERUMAC?" Buck asked.

"Several thousand dollars," Kale said.

"Wow," Toni said. "It'd take a lot of pizza deliveries!"

"So, another person was flying a drone in the park," Buck stated. "I've seen three of them now."

"Really?" Kayla said. "Where was the third one?"

"In the campground," Buck said. "An OR-213, chasing a moose."

"You didn't fly yours in the campground, did you, Kale?" Kayla said with alarm.

"No," Kale stated.

"I didn't think so," Kayla said, then turned to Buck. "Let's get back to the wolves. Do they attack the elk?"

"Watch," Buck said. He reached over, closed out of the site about the drone, and brought up Shoop's video again. It was still frozen, and Buck could now see how Kale easily identified the GERUMAC. The grayish halo was made by the four black rotors rapidly spinning. He could barely make out the two landing skids below the blades, and he knew the red speck was the payload claw.

"I guess whoever was flying that," Buck said, "was following the wolves. Do you know how fast it goes?"

"Yes," Kale stated.

"How fast, Kale?" his sister said impatiently.

"Top speed is about sixty-seven miles per hour," Kale answered without hesitation.

"No problem keeping up with a wolf," Buck said. He clicked the mouse to start the video again, but his mind was racing. Even watching the wolves take down the elk didn't keep his attention.

That's how the kibble was dropped, Buck thought. *From that GERUMAC!*

TAKE 13:

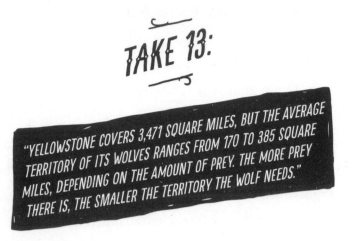

"YELLOWSTONE COVERS 3,471 SQUARE MILES, BUT THE AVERAGE TERRITORY OF ITS WOLVES RANGES FROM 170 TO 385 SQUARE MILES, DEPENDING ON THE AMOUNT OF PREY. THE MORE PREY THERE IS, THE SMALLER THE TERRITORY THE WOLF NEEDS."

"I'm wondering something, Kale," Buck said. "If I wanted to feed my dog without going outside, could I just grab some kibble and drop it in his food bowl?"

"No," Kale answered.

"You'll get better answers if you don't ask yes–no questions," Kayla quietly told Buck.

"Why not?" Buck rephrased his question.

"The GERUMAC's payload claw couldn't hold a bunch of kibble," Kale said. "It would all fall out. It would have to be in a box or a baggie or something."

Just then, a phone rang from outside, and they heard Dad answer it.

"Okay, I will," Dad said, and soon he stepped into the Green Beast.

"Kayla, Kale, your mom says you need to head home," Dad said.

"That's in Oregon," Kale said.

"Head back to your RV," Dad corrected himself.

"Kale can be quite literal sometimes," Kayla explained.

"That's okay," Dad said. "Then there's no confusion."

The kids all said goodbye to one another. As soon as Kayla and Kale went out the door, Buck turned to Toni.

"That drone must have dropped the kibble somehow," he said. Then, without saying another word, Buck suddenly jumped up and raced out the door. Kayla and Kale had already left the campsite and were walking down the road.

"Wait a second," he called out, jogging quickly toward them. "Do you think Toni and I could go with you tomorrow to the drone competition?"

"Sure," said Kayla, "but we'll have to ask our parents first."

"Us too," Buck said. "Give me a call when you find out."

"Okay," Kayla said. The twins continued on down the road, and Buck headed toward where Dad was splitting some wood. Shoop was sitting in a camp chair with his feet crossed on the edge of the fire ring.

"Thought we'd have a campfire tonight," Dad said, "since we don't have to get up early tomorrow."

"Okay," Buck said, "but I was wondering. Could Toni and I go with Kale and Kayla tomorrow to the drone competition? I'd love to see him fly, and Abby said there were classes for beginners. Maybe I could take one."

"Who's Abby?" Dad said.

"That backpacker we talked to today," Buck said.

"Oh yeah," Dad said.

"Can we?" Buck asked again.

"I don't know, Buck," Dad said.

"It'll give the kids something to do while we edit," Shoop said.

"I'll think about it," Dad said. "Help me stack this wood by the fire ring when I'm finished." Dad split several more

pieces. As Buck helped carry the wood to the fire ring, his father's phone rang. Dad answered it. Whoever it was talked for a while.

"Yes, that would be wonderful. They would love to," Dad finally said into the phone. "Buck heard they have beginner lessons. Would he and Toni be able to take one?"

"That would be cool," Buck whispered to Shoop.

"How much are they?" Dad asked.

Dad paused for a moment, and then continued. "Okay, then. They'll meet you down by Philo's at seven thirty so you don't have to loop through the whole campground again. Thank you.

"You're all set," Dad said as he put the phone in his back pocket. He pulled his wallet from his other pocket and handed Buck two twenty-dollar bills. "This is for the lessons."

"Thanks, Dad!" Buck said.

Buck stuffed the twenties in his pocket, then charged back into the Green Beast.

"Dad said we can go with the Kolsons tomorrow and also take a lesson," Buck said.

"That will be fun," Toni said, her eyes never leaving the computer. The screen was frozen at the beginning of the elk kill.

"I've looked carefully through the entire elk kill shot," she said. "That's the only time you can see the drone. Shoop kept moving the camera to see the wolves better."

"Maybe we'll find out something more at the competition," Buck said. "Whoever it was may be competing."

"Abby said that tomorrow was for juniors," Toni said. "I doubt this guy was a kid."

"Jason Dekster is," Buck said. "Philo said he was fifteen, and his truck was at Slough Creek."

"*Maybe* his truck was there," Toni corrected.

"Whatever," Buck said, "but he's one of two suspects."

"Two?" Toni asked. "Who's the other? You're not thinking Kalc, are you? He doesn't own a GERUMAC."

"No, but Abby might," Buck said.

"They were going backpacking," Toni said. "We saw them leave."

"Well, they wouldn't fly in front of us," Buck s "They could have been planning on it, but

along, so they pretended they were leaving the drone and then came back for it once we left."

"I guess that's possible," Toni said. "They had plenty of time."

"Let's call Isabel and ask her what kind of drone they had," Buck said.

"We need to tell Lobo about the GERUMAC too," Toni added. The two rushed outside.

"I need to use your phone," Buck said to Dad.

Dad slid the phone from his pocket. "Who are you calling? The Kolsons?"

"No, Isabel and Lobo," Buck said. "We think a drone dropped the poisoned kibble."

"Wait a second," Dad said, still holding on to the phone. "What are you talking about?"

"Come here," Toni said. "We'll show you."

Dad and Shoop followed the kids into the camper, and the four of them crowded around Toni's computer. She showed them the frozen image of the wolves and injured elk and pointed out the drone. Then she brought up the website about the GERUMAC.

"Kale identified it instantly," Buck said. "Now that you know what it looks like, look at it again in the video."

Toni pulled up the frozen image again. Shoop and Dad both looked at it carefully.

"You're right," Dad said. "It does look like a drone."

"It can carry cargo and has an automatic release," Buck said. "We think it may have been following Odin and released the poisoned kibble near him."

"There are only two things we don't know," Toni said. "Who was flying it and how the drone held the kibble. Kale said it would have to be in a box or a baggie or something. Not just a bunch of loose kibble pieces."

"Did you tell them about Odin?" Dad asked sharply. "Lobo asked you not to."

"No," Buck said. "I told him I wanted to feed my dog without leaving the house."

Dad shook his head, grinning. "You don't even have a dog. They make you sneeze."

"That's it!" Buck blurted out so loudly, it took everyone by surprise. "Shoop, how many tissues do you have in your pocket?"

"What?" Shoop said. "Just one. It's used, though."

Shoop reached in his pocket and pulled out a wadded-up tissue. But when he did, a lens cloth and a second tissue fell to the floor. He started to pick them up, but Buck grabbed his hand.

"Don't touch it!" Buck commanded. "And drop the other one, too. I don't know which is which, but one of them may have cyanide on it."

Buck pushed past the men and went into the kitchen. He opened a drawer and pulled out a ziplock baggie and a pair of tongs. Then, returning to Toni's room, he used the tongs to pick up both tissues, along with the lens cloth, and put them in the baggie.

"Your lens cloth might have gotten cyanide on it, too," Buck said, "since it was also in your pocket."

"I thought I had just dropped my tissue," Shoop said, shaking his head. "I didn't realize I was picking up a piece of evidence. So, you think the kibble was tied up in a tissue?"

"Probably not tied," Buck said. "I think the kibble was just wrapped in the tissue, so when it was dropped, the kibble would scatter and the tissue would just blow away."

"Good thinking!" Dad said. He looked at his watch and then began punching in a number on his phone. "It's almost five. I hope Lobo doesn't leave early on Fridays."

Everyone was quiet, looking at Dad as he put his phone to his ear.

"Chuck, this is Dan Bray. I have some important information about the wolf killing. Please give me a call as soon as possible."

When Dad finished giving his phone number, he ended the call. "I got his voice mail," he said. "He may not even hear it until Monday. I'll try Isabel."

Dad punched in another number and left almost the same message and turned to the others.

"I'll try again in the morning."

"That may be too late," Toni said in alarm. "What if whoever it was tries to poison the other wolves?"

"Maybe Philo would be able to radio in to the rangers," Buck said. "We'll go ask him."

Buck and Toni burst out of the Green Beast and raced up the road. Philo was standing beside a pickup with a camper in the truck bed, explaining that the campground was full.

"It fills up pretty fast on Fridays," Philo said. "How long were you planning on staying?"

"For a week," the man in the pickup said.

"Well, your best bet for a campsite in the park would be Sunday. Lots of people leave then, but get here early. There will be a line."

As the pickup left, Philo turned to Buck and Toni.

"So where's the fire?" he asked.

"What?" Buck said. "A fire?"

"That's what people ask when someone is in a rush," Philo explained.

"Can you call the rangers on your radio?" Buck asked.

"No," Philo replied. "I can only listen in. Why?"

"We saw something on the video that Shoop shot today that looks like it may be involved with . . ." Buck suddenly realized he was about to reveal what he promised he wouldn't. But Toni quickly intervened.

"The coyotes being poisoned," Toni finished.

"We tried to call Lobo but got his voice mail," Buck added almost before Toni stopped talking.

"And we're worried whoever it is may kill more animals," Toni said quickly, too.

"Whoa—slow down. I can't listen to you both at the same time," Philo said, and looked at Toni. "Ladies first."

"We need a phone number for a ranger," Toni said. "Lobo and Isabel didn't answer their phones."

"Got one right here," Philo said, pulling his phone from his pocket. "An emergency phone number. But I'll call them. I'm not supposed to give that number out."

"Tell them they need to call Dad," Buck said. He started to give Philo the number, but the man put his hand up.

"I won't remember it," Philo said. "But I've got it on your registration envelope."

The two kids followed the old man into the shed. He pulled an envelope from a box and placed his call.

"This is Philo East at Mammoth Campground," he said. "We've got a camper here that has some info about the coyote killings. The man's name is Dan Bray. He's camping at site number twenty-two."

Philo read Dad's phone number off the envelope and ended the call. "They'll give your dad a call. So, what is it that you saw?"

Buck looked at Toni, wondering how they should answer, and was relieved that another RV had pulled in and stopped outside the shed.

"This happens every Friday about this time," Philo said. "Would you guys run that sign up to the main entrance for me? I haven't had a chance."

Philo pointed to a sign nailed to a sawhorse that said CAMPGROUND FULL—NO VACANCIES.

"Sure," Buck said.

"Thanks," Philo said. "Just put it smack in the middle. People will have room to come and go on either side of it."

As Philo headed toward the RV, Buck and Toni carried the sign to the entrance. Then, cutting the corner and going behind the shed to avoid answering any more of Philo's questions, they raced back to their campsite. Dad and Shoop were sitting in the Green Beast, the phone on the table on speaker.

"I'll stop by tomorrow and pick up the tissues," Lobo's voice could be heard saying as Buck and Toni quietly sat down. "I'd like to see that part of the video, too."

"That will be fine," Dad stated. "The kids are going into town, but Shoop and I will be here."

"Okay," Lobo said. "Anything else?"

"Yes," Buck blurted out. "What about the other wolves? What if the guy drops more poison?"

"I'll put an order out to immediately close off Slough Creek Road," Lobo said. "I'll also have extra patrols in areas near other wolf packs. We'll do everything we can to protect them."

"Good," Buck said. "That makes me feel better."

"Well, I'm just glad you and Toni figured this out," Lobo said. "That was some really good detective work."

"Thanks," Buck and Toni said in unison.

TAKE 14:

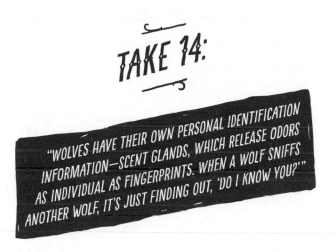

"WOLVES HAVE THEIR OWN PERSONAL IDENTIFICATION INFORMATION—SCENT GLANDS, WHICH RELEASE ODORS AS INDIVIDUAL AS FINGERPRINTS. WHEN A WOLF SNIFFS ANOTHER WOLF, IT'S JUST FINDING OUT, 'DO I KNOW YOU?'"

"I think you have some homework you haven't completed, Buck," Dad said as he put away his phone. "Go take care of that while I get the grill going. After dinner, we can all enjoy the fire together."

Buck groaned but went into Toni's room as the others went outside. Within ten minutes, he had finished his homework and sent it to Mrs. Webster. Instantly, Mrs. Webster came online to chat.

Toni said you were going wolf watching today, she wrote. *Did you see any?*

Yes, Buck wrote back, *four adults and three pups.*

Send pictures, Mrs. Webster wrote.

I'll e-mail some of a black bear with cubs and the Bighorn sheep that we saw, Buck wrote, *but the wolves were too far away for me to take pictures with my camera.*

Buck started looking through the images he had downloaded earlier, but seeing two photos he had forgotten about, he quickly wrote to Mrs. Webster. *I'll send pictures later—dinner's ready.* He pushed send and logged out.

"Hey, Toni," Buck called out through the window. "Come here a second, would you, please?"

"All right," Toni called back, "but I'm not doing your homework for you."

Toni came into the room and sat down in her chair.

"What do you need help with?" she asked. "You're usually good in math."

"I don't need help," Buck said. "I've already sent in my homework. I want to show you this."

Buck brought up a very out-of-focus photo of a pickup truck with a camper shell over the bed.

"The truck that passed us when we first saw the sheep

was black," Buck said.

"So here we go with another black truck," Toni said in exasperation.

"Just listen," Buck said. "Philo said the Deksters left just after we did. When we slowed down to look at the sheep, they passed us and got to Slough Creek before we did. That was their truck at the gate, I'm certain."

"That picture doesn't prove it was their truck," Toni said. "Besides, we would have followed them and seen them turn down Slough Creek Road."

"No," Buck said. "We stopped to video sheep, so they would have gotten way ahead of us. Jason and his dad had hours to fly that drone around looking for wolves. Then, when the pack went out to hunt, they spotted Odin and dropped the poisoned kibble near him."

"Kale said the GERUMAC could fly for an hour," Toni stated, "not hours."

"On one set of batteries," Buck said. "I'm sure they would have spares. But what I want you to look at is the next picture. I caught part of the license plate. It's the same color, but I can't make out what it says."

Buck brought up another picture. The truck was almost past the SUV in this picture, and it was easy to see a blue-and-white license plate. But, as with the other photo, it was very blurred.

"I can't tell about the first part, but the last two look like an *N* and an *R* to me," Buck said.

Toni looked at the photo, zoomed in, and zoomed back out.

"I agree there's an *N*," she said. "But the last letter—it could be an *R*, but it looks more like a *K* to me."

"Think about it, Toni. What are the chances of another black truck, identical to the Deksters' except for the last letter of its license plate, just happening to drive past us?" Buck said. "It's more likely that it's an *R* and it *is* the Deksters' truck."

"The license of the truck at the gate was all muddy," Toni said. "This one is clean."

"It got muddy when they drove through all those puddles on Slough Creek Road," Buck argued. "Just like Isabel's."

Toni looked at the two pictures again. "Maybe, but

if you had looked carefully, you would have noticed the cab's windows were down, and you can see in."

"So?" Buck said.

"Take a look—you can't see who it is, but you can tell there's only one person in the truck," she said. "So it couldn't be the Deksters."

"Maybe Jason drove by himself."

"Jason is only fifteen and has a learner's permit," Toni argued. "His dad probably wouldn't let him drive by himself. It's illegal."

"It's illegal to fly drones in the park, and I'm certain Jason was flying the OR-213," Buck said. "It's also illegal to poison wolves, but that's obviously not stopping somebody."

"That's true," Toni said just as Dad stuck his head in the camper's door.

"Dinner's ready," he said. "Did you get your homework done?"

"Yeah," Buck answered. He and Toni went outside, but all through dinner and then afterward in front of the campfire, Buck was quiet.

"A penny for your thoughts," Dad finally said to him.

"I just keep thinking about Odin," Buck said. "I know that drone had something to do with his death, but I can't figure out who was flying it, or where he was flying it from."

"Well, I'm sure the rangers will figure it out," Dad assured him. "You guys helped them out a bunch, though. Lobo was really appreciative."

"And you might have saved more wolves from being killed," Shoop added.

"I know," Buck said, but there was still an edge of disappointment in his voice.

It was growing dark and the embers were glowing in the fire ring when Buck suddenly jumped up.

"I forgot," he said. "I told Mrs. Webster I'd send her some pictures. Toni, come help me pick out which ones."

Toni got up and followed Buck to the Green Beast.

"What did you remember?" she asked as they sat down. "I know you wouldn't be that concerned about sending Mrs. Webster any photos."

Buck turned on the computer and brought up two

photos side by side. One was a close-up of the grizzly track with his hand beside it. The other was taken before Buck squatted down.

"What do you see?" Buck said.

"A grizzly track," Toni said skeptically.

"And what else?"

"Boot tracks."

"Exactly. All we have to do is match the tracks," Buck said. "We'll go over to the Deksters' campsite and look for boot tracks with five circles lined up in an arc near the ball of the foot, three more on the heel, and zigzag lines everywhere else. That will prove that it was them."

"There's only one set of tracks," Toni said. "The left foot landed before the grizzly track, and the right foot almost stepped on it. And there's the heel of the left foot again—it's almost out of the picture."

"So?" Buck said.

"So, there was only one person," Toni said. "Not both Jason and his dad."

"They wouldn't walk in single file," Buck pointed out. "One set of their tracks wouldn't be in the picture."

"Yeah, but there was also only one sandwich wrapper in the fire ring," Toni said.

"Maybe the other put his sandwich wrapper in his pocket," Buck countered.

"And maybe Jason laid down in the truck when they drove past us so we wouldn't see him," Toni said sarcastically. "I'm telling you. I don't think it was him."

"Well, I'm going to go look at their boot tracks, anyway," Buck said stubbornly.

"You won't be able to see anything in the dark," Toni said, "and you can't go snooping around in someone's campsite with flashlights."

"Then I'll go in the morning before we go with the Kolsons."

———◆———

For the second night in a row, Buck tossed and turned. He dreamt about wolves flying around in drones, buzzing past geysers and mud pots, and a red fox grabbing kibble from a tissue left in a fire ring. An injured elk walked along a fallen tree across a spring of boiling bright blue water, wobbled, and started to fall. Buck sat straight up in alarm, breathing hard. He looked around, at first not knowing where he was, but then heard Dad snoring softly on the bed behind him and realized he had been dreaming. Shoop rolled over but didn't wake.

Buck lay back down. *Whoever was flying the drone was there before we went to the ranger station,* he thought. *And he couldn't fly it in the parking lot. Too much of a chance that someone would see him. He had to be in the campground.* Buck sat back up again. *The boot prints only went one direction—in, not out. Whoever it was, he was in the campground when we were! Had to have been. The truck was still there when we walked to the campground. But it was gone when we walked back out. I was so upset about Odin, I didn't even notice the truck had left! And I never even thought about looking for tracks coming back out.*

Buck quietly got out of bed and pulled on some sweatpants. Then he tiptoed over to Toni's door and slowly opened it.

"Toni?" he whispered. There was no answer.

Buck went in the room and shut the door behind him. He could hear Toni's steady breathing from her bunk above the desk. He sat down at the computer, and turned it on. The sound of the computer opening up seemed incredibly loud, and the light from the screen hurt his eyes. Toni instantly leaned over the bunk and looked down at him.

"What are you doing?" she asked.

"Sorry," Buck said. "I didn't mean to wake you. I just thought of something."

"Do you have any idea what time it is?" Toni said.

Buck looked at the computer. "Twelve thirty."

"Ohhh," Toni moaned. "Go back to bed!"

"I will," Buck said. "In just a second."

Toni flopped back over onto her bunk, turned toward the wall, and pulled the covers over her head. But Buck continued bringing up Shoop's video, then fast-forwarded until he saw himself skipping a stone. He watched himself balance on the tree across the creek and back, and then climb up onto the picnic table. He saw himself looking through the binoculars, discovering Odin's lifeless body.

He didn't see anything unusual but decided to watch it one more time before going back to bed.

When he reversed it, he went back a little too far and saw the last of the elk kill, where the magpie grabbed a bite from the carcass.

"That's enough to give anybody nightmares," Buck said to himself.

"Shhh," Toni said from under the covers. "I'm trying to sleep."

"Sorry," Buck said, and went back to watching. Shoop had evidently turned off the camera as Geri returned to eat after chasing away a coyote. Without any gap, the video went from the wolf eating to a pan shot of the Slough Creek Campground. Starting with the fallen tree, the scene slowly moved to the fire ring, and on past into the woods where the fox had run. Buck quickly reached out and froze the image.

"I can't believe it!" he said. "There he is! He's hiding in the bushes!"

TAKE 15:

SATURDAY, MAY 17

When Buck discovered the man hiding behind the bushes at the campground, he started to tell Toni, but she had fallen back to sleep. So he turned off the computer and went back to bed. He didn't think he'd get to sleep, but the next thing he knew, Dad was waking him. Toni was spreading peanut butter and jelly on slices of bread, and Shoop was sitting on the couch, putting fresh batteries in the camera.

"I let you sleep as long as possible," Dad said, "but you need to get up and get dressed now."

"Toni," Buck said. "A little privacy, please."

"Oh, so privacy is important now, huh?" Toni said, but she put down the knife, went into her room, and closed the door.

"What was that all about?" Dad asked.

"Nothing," Buck said, realizing Toni hadn't told anyone that he had gone in her room to use the computer in the middle of the night. He quickly dressed, and then, knocking on Toni's door, he grabbed his gray hoodie and went out to the campground's restroom. When he returned, he ate his breakfast and brushed his teeth.

"Are you ready?" he asked Toni.

"It's only seven. We don't need to be at Philo's until seven thirty," Toni answered. "Oh, yeah, I forgot. Time doesn't seem to matter to you, does it?"

Both Dad and Shoop looked at each other questioningly, but Shoop just shrugged. Buck was relieved Dad didn't ask him anything more.

"We were planning on taking a walk around the campground before we leave, remember?" Buck said to Toni. "To look for tracks."

"Oh yeah," Toni said without much enthusiasm, and put the sandwiches in plastic baggies.

"Take my phone with you today," Shoop said. "It's in the kitchen drawer."

"Okay," Toni said. She held a sandwich out to Buck. "Here's yours, Buck. I've got water in my pack's water bladder, but you'll need to bring your own."

"I wasn't going to take my backpack," Buck said, not taking the sandwich. "I was just going to clip a water bottle on my belt."

"Or ask me to carry it," Toni complained. "You never carry anything." She grabbed her backpack, stuffed both sandwiches in it, and stepped out of the Green Beast. As Buck started to fill his water bottle, Dad put his hand on his shoulder.

"I want you to behave yourself today," he said sternly. "I don't know what you and Toni are bickering about, but it better stop."

Buck started to say that she started it, but stopped himself, realizing Toni had a right to be irritated at him.

"Toni and I are fine," he said to his dad. "Nothing is

going on."

As Buck stepped out of the camper, he heard Shoop chuckling inside. "Yeah right," he said. "There's always something going on with those two."

Toni had gone on ahead and was already two campsites up the road. Buck clipped his water bottle onto his belt and ran to catch up with her.

"I'm sorry I came in your room last night," he stated, "but I woke up wondering about something, and you won't believe what I saw."

"What?" Toni said. She still didn't sound overly enthusiastic.

"When we were at the Slough Creek Campground, there was a person hiding in the bushes!" Buck said.

"Really? Where?" Toni asked. Now she sounded more interested.

"Back where the fox ran," Buck said. "I couldn't see his face. He was ducked down behind some bushes, wearing a gray hoodie. I could see his shoulders. It looked like there were black straps or something on them. It could have been the backpack for the GERUMAC."

"Why didn't you show me?" Toni asked.

"By time I saw it, you'd gone back to sleep," Buck said. "I didn't want to wake you again."

"Why didn't you say something to Shoop and your dad this morning?" Toni asked. "They could tell Lobo."

"Because we don't know who it was for certain. I'm trying not to jump to conclusions," Buck said. "I want to look at Jason's boot prints first. Then we'll know for sure."

"If it is Jason's boot print, the only thing we'd really know is that Jason was there, just like we were there," Toni said. "It still wouldn't prove he poisoned Odin."

They had reached the registration area. A blue car pulling a pop-up camper trailer was stopped in front of the shed, and Philo was standing next to the driver's window.

"No," Philo said. "It's just like the sign says. The camp-ground is full."

"Can I just wait here until checkout?" the driver said. "If someone leaves, then I'll be able to take their spot."

"You can do that," Philo said, "but I don't have anybody scheduled to leave today."

Because Philo was busy, Buck and Toni started to walk on past, but Philo turned and smiled.

"Good morning!" he said. "You're up and about early. Anything you kids need?"

"No, just going for a walk," Buck said, "and then to Gardiner with the Kolsons to watch the drone competition."

As he spoke, a black truck came slowly driving down the hill from the upper tier. The driver's side window was rolled down, and a young teen was at the wheel. A man sat in the passenger seat beside him. Buck kept his eye on the truck as it went past and stopped at the main road.

"See," the man in the blue car called out to Philo. "I knew someone would be leaving. We can have their site."

"Have a good time," Philo said to the kids, then turned back toward the driver.

"Just because people leave, it doesn't mean they're checking out. Those people happen to be going into town for the day, but they'll be back tonight."

Buck and Toni walked on.

"That was the Deksters that left!" Buck said when

they were out of earshot of Philo. "And their license was covered in mud!"

"You're kidding!" Toni said, but then changed her tone. "But, you know, a lot of people's are. Look at all the puddles here in the campground. That rain the other night muddied up everything."

"Yeah, but did you see what Jason was wearing?" Buck said. "A gray hoodie!"

"I saw," Toni said. "You're wearing one, too."

"But you know I wasn't the one flying a drone," Buck said. "Jason was. I'm certain."

"But where was his dad all that time?" Toni asked.

"Probably hiding too," Buck said. "He just didn't get caught on camera."

"You're not being very scientific," Toni said.

They had reached the upper tier and hurried over to the Deksters' campsite. "I'm glad they left early," Buck said. "We'll be able to look around better."

"I don't really like going into someone's campsite uninvited," Toni said, standing at the entrance of the site's driveway.

"We won't be in there long," Buck said. He walked into the driveway, looking down at the ground. Toni reluctantly followed, but neither went far.

"Here's a boot print," Toni said, "but it's not the same as the one in your picture."

Buck looked at the print. It had no circles at all. Only stripes. "That's one person's. Let's look for the other's."

Buck walked on over toward the picnic table. "There's a print here with circles," he said, "but it's too smudged to tell."

"I've got one with circles too," Toni said. "Do you still have the pictures on your camera? We need to compare."

Buck pulled the camera from his pocket and brought up the picture with a bear track between his hand and a boot track. He looked carefully at the boot track on the camera and then back at the print on the ground. The circles were all in the wrong places, and instead of zigzags, there were fans of straight lines coming from each circle, like sun rays.

"It's not it," Toni said. "So Jason is ruled out."

"Not necessarily," Buck said. "Maybe he just wears

sneakers around the campsite, and put on his hiking boots before walking into Slough Creek Campground."

"Come on, Buck," Toni said. "You're really stretching it."

"No," Buck said. "That's what Abby was doing, changing from sneakers to hiking boots."

"I didn't see her do that," Toni said.

"That's because she was done before you came out of the outhouse," Buck said. "Well, let's go. The Kolsons will be meeting us soon."

"Aren't we going to call your dad?" Toni asked. "He can let Lobo know."

"Know what?" Buck said. "You keep saying we don't know anything yet."

"We should let him know about the guy hiding at the campground," Toni said. "And that Jason is ruled out. No sense for Lobo to waste his time chasing after someone who wasn't there."

"He could have been," Buck argued.

"Highly improbable," Toni said. She took off her backpack and unzipped the main compartment, but it only took a second for her to pull her hand back out.

"I forgot to get Shoop's phone out of the drawer," she said. "We might have time to run back and tell them."

Toni barely had the words out when the Kolsons' RV came driving up the road toward them.

TAKE 16:

"WOLVES DON'T GET SNOW DAYS, AND THEY DON'T HIBERNATE. THEIR THICK FUR KEEPS THEM WARM AND DRY AS THEY CURL UP AND SLEEP NEAR ONE ANOTHER IN THE OPEN AIR."

The RV pulled up beside Buck and Toni. Kayla opened the door.

"Are you guys ready?"

"Yeah," Buck said. He and Toni hopped in.

"What were you guys doing?" Kayla asked as they sat down with Kale at the table.

"Just looking for tracks," Buck answered.

The RV drove around the bend and down the hill. As they turned onto the main road, Toni called up to Mrs. Kolson.

"Could I use your phone, please?" she asked. "I forgot mine and need to call my dad."

"I'm sorry, sweetie," Mrs. Kolson answered. "Our batteries are completely dead. We never thought about the campground not having electric hookups, and we don't have a generator. We're trying to get Kale's drone batteries all charged up as we drive."

Buck looked toward the front of the RV. A small charger holding four rectangular batteries was plugged into the RV's power outlet.

"Is it an emergency?" Mr. Kolson asked Toni. "I can turn around right up here at that turnout."

"No," Toni said. "No big deal. It can wait until we get back."

It was a beautiful drive, going steadily downhill on the twisty road that followed the Gardner River as it cut through the canyon, winding around cliffs and mountains. They had driven about ten minutes when Mrs. Kolson called back, "We're out of Wyoming and in Montana now."

"So, are we out of the park now?" Toni asked.

"No," Mr. Kolson answered, "not for a few more miles.

The park's boundary is at the edge of town."

It wasn't long before they drove past a rustic-looking building where rangers were stopping cars going the opposite direction. Ahead, a tall but narrow stone archway spanned the road. Words were engraved in the stone across the top.

"There's the Roosevelt Arch—the park's northern entrance or exit," Mrs. Kolson said, and then read aloud, "'For the benefit and enjoyment of the people.'"

"We'll come back and get pictures later," Mr. Kolson said as he drove through the arch. "The school's right there."

Just past the arch, a stone wall edged the school's football field and track. On the other side of the field, vehicles were streaming into a parking lot that separated the playing field from the long, stone school building. Mr. Kolson drove to the back of the line.

"Look," Kayla called out. "Elk are grazing on the football field!"

"And look at that," Toni said, pointing toward the building. "A grizzly!"

Buck was watching the elk but now whipped his head around the other direction. Both Toni and Kayla laughed when they saw the look of disappointment on his face. A large statue of a grizzly on some big rocks stood near the flagpole in front of the school.

"You got me on that one— the statue is pretty cool." Buck grinned. "But do you think the school spelled its name wrong?"

"No," Toni said. "In one of the brochures it said that the town of Gardiner is spelled with the letter *i*, but there's no *i* in the river's name."

"You've probably already pointed that out to Mrs. Webster, haven't you?" Buck said. Toni just grinned and nodded.

The parking lot was crowded, both with cars pulling into the few remaining spots and people heading toward the school. Some had on small backpacks, others carried various sizes of cases and boxes, and some just had their drones in their hands. Mr. Kolson drove slowly, stopping frequently to let people walk past.

"Buck, did you notice?" Toni said. "Just about every

kid—and a lot of the adults, too—is wearing a gray hoodie."

"All the contestants get them," Kayla said.

"I guess I'll blend in," Buck said as Mr. Kolson found a place to park the RV.

As soon as the vehicle came to a complete stop, Kale hurried through a door in the back. He returned holding a gray hoodie sweatshirt, a cardboard case, and a new package of double-A batteries. He put the case on the table and pulled the sweatshirt over his head. Embroidered on the front was a small drone. Above it were the letters *U.S.A.,* and below, *U.F.O.*

"Unidentified flying objects?" Buck asked.

"No," Kale said.

"It stands for Unmanned Flights Organization," Kayla said. "They're the ones putting on the competition."

Kale opened the case. Inside, protected by foam rubber, was a white drone, about a foot in diameter. It had two red rotors and two white ones, all inside white protective plastic rings. Several grass stains were on the rotors and rings.

"Is there a reason that the rotors are two different colors?" Toni asked.

"Yes," Kale said.

"Kale, tell them why there are two different rotor colors," Mrs. Kolson said from the front.

"So you can tell which way it's going," Kale said. "Red's in back. If it's moving with the red in front, you're actually flying backward, and your camera's pointed the wrong way."

Kale went to the front of the RV, unplugged the battery charger, and brought it back to the table. He put three of the batteries in the drone's case, then took out the drone. Turning it upside down, he inserted a battery into a slot and plugged the battery's wire into another wire on the drone.

"What's that?" Buck asked, pointing to a small rectangular piece of plastic below the battery.

"The camera," Kale said. Then, showing Buck a small round piece of glass no bigger than the head of a pin, he added, "That's the lens."

Setting the drone on the table, Kale took the controller

from the case and loaded three of the double-A batteries into it.

"This joystick makes it go up and down, that one back and forth," Kale said, moving the joysticks around with his thumbs. When he flipped on the power switch, the controller beeped, and a small screen lit up with various digital displays.

"Don't you hook it up to your phone?" Buck asked. When he only got "No" for an answer, Buck rephrased his question. "Why don't you?"

"The AeroSpurt RC isn't that fancy," Kale answered, "and my OR-213 is too small for the competition."

"Kale's OR-213 uses a phone," Kayla added, "but he has to use our mom's. Our parents won't let us have our own phones."

"My dad won't either," Buck said.

"Neither will Shoop," Toni said.

Kale picked up the drone and flipped on another switch. He put the drone back on the table, then he picked up the controller and pushed one of the joysticks slightly forward. The drone's rotors started spinning, and it slowly lifted from the table. It hovered there for a few seconds, then flew in a small circle above the table and then lowered, landing back on the table. Kale turned off the switch on the drone, then flipped the power switch on the controller, and the screen went blank.

"All working fine," he announced. He put everything back in the case. Exiting the RV, they all headed toward the school entrance.

"Cool-looking school," Toni stated as they walked past the grizzly statue and entered the school lobby. A gigantic octagonal planter filled with a variety of plants and wooden benches encircling it took up the middle of the lobby. Heavy wood beams stretched across the lofted ceiling, and tall windows looked out at the bear statue and the Roosevelt Arch. Kale was already preregistered, so he and his family headed across the lobby to the gym doors. Toni and Buck got in a short line at the school's reception counter beside the front door.

"Are you competing?" the woman behind the counter asked when it was their turn. A name tag on her shirt said JANET, GARDINER SCHOOL SECRETARY.

"No," Buck said. "We're here to watch a friend compete. But we want to sign up for a beginner's class."

"There are three," Janet said. "What time does your friend compete?"

"I don't know," Buck said.

"Do you know what grade he's in?" Janet asked.

"Sixth," Toni answered.

"Then he'll be in the ten-o'clock rounds. Opening comments are at eight thirty in the gym," Janet told them. "Grades two through five compete at nine, middle schoolers at ten, high schoolers at eleven. There's a lunch break at noon, and awards are after lunch at a quarter to one. So, do you want to take the nine o'clock or eleven o'clock class?"

"Nine," Buck said, then he turned to Toni. "I want to see Jason fly, too."

"It'll be twenty dollars each," Janet said, handing them forms to fill out. Toni started filling out one of the forms as Buck reached in his pocket.

"Wow," he said as he handed the secretary the money, "that's an awesome photograph!"

Toni looked up. On the wall behind the secretary was a photo of a real grizzly sitting down, leaning against the rocks that the grizzly statue stood on.

"Cool," she said. "Looks like he found a friend! Does that happen often?"

"Not often," Janet said, smiling, "and I'm glad it doesn't. We missed a half day of school because we couldn't unload the buses until it decided to move."

"Toni, we'll have to tell Mrs. Webster that kids here get *bear days* off instead of snow days," Buck said.

"Put your e-mail address on the form," Janet said, chuckling. "I'll e-mail the photo to you so you can show her."

"Thanks!" Buck said.

When Buck finished filling out his form, the secretary handed them each a name tag and a gray T-shirt with the U.F.O. logo printed on the front. "A T-shirt comes with taking a class," she stated.

Both kids thanked the secretary. As they walked away, Toni spoke to Buck, "The restrooms are over there. I'm going to go change into this."

"Stuff mine in your backpack," Buck said, handing Toni his T-shirt. "Beginners get T-shirts. I don't want to look like a beginner."

As Toni went into the restroom, Buck peeled the backing off the name tag and stuck it on his hoodie, purposely covering the spot where the U.F.O. logo was on the competitors hoodies. When Toni came back out in her new T-shirt, the two went into the gym and found the Kolsons.

TAKE 17:

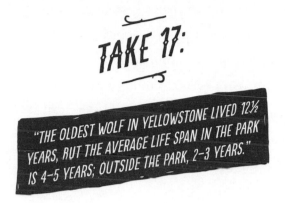

"THE OLDEST WOLF IN YELLOWSTONE LIVED 12½ YEARS, BUT THE AVERAGE LIFE SPAN IN THE PARK IS 4–5 YEARS; OUTSIDE THE PARK, 2–3 YEARS."

Five people sat on folding chairs in the middle of the gym, a microphone on a stand in front of them. A hush quieted the audience in the bleachers as one of the people, a man, stood and approached the mic.

"Good morning," he announced. "I'm Mike Orso, the principal of Gardiner School, where all two hundred young people in our little mountain town, as well as kids from Mammoth, get a fantastic education from kindergarten through twelfth grade."

Mr. Orso paused as several of the families in the

bleachers cheered and clapped, yelling, "Go Bruins!"

"I want to welcome you to the Unmanned Flights Organization's annual competition, and we are honored to host this year's events. I understand there are competitors here from twelve different states, as well as two from right here in Gardiner and one from Mammoth."

Again, some families cheered. Mr. Orso put his hand up to quiet them.

"There are just a few announcements I want to make before the competition begins," Mr. Orso continued. "First, please remember there is to be no flying of drones outside the building. We are only two miles from the airport, and the Federal Aviation Administration prohibits flying drones within five miles. Plus, Yellowstone's border is really close. In fact, the boundary actually goes right through the middle of our shop classroom. As I'm sure you're aware, flying is banned in the park. As you know, anyone breaking either of those rules could face federal prosecution."

"That hasn't stopped Jason," Buck whispered to Toni.

"Shhh," Toni said. "I want to hear."

"Also, there will be no flying anyplace inside the building except in the gym, where the competition takes place, and in the cafeteria, where flying classes take place. Anyone breaking that rule will be disqualified from this competition. Everyone is on their own for lunch. There's a soda machine in the teachers' lounge down the hall past the cafeteria, and a drinking fountain just outside the gym doors between the restrooms. I think that's about it. I wish everyone the best of luck, and most importantly have fun! And now, I want to introduce . . ."

The principal stopped talking as the secretary came hurrying through the gym doors. She quickly jogged over to the principal and quietly talked with him. Then Mr. Orso turned back to the crowd.

"I just heard that someone left the playground gate open, and bison have wandered in."

There was a chuckle from the crowd and a buzz of voices.

"That may be an unusual thing for most of you folks to hear," Mr. Orso spoke over the voices, "but if you noticed the elk on the football field this morning, you'd realize the animals don't know where the park boundaries are."

Again the crowd laughed.

"So, we've got the maintenance director out there on a tractor trying to move them out. . . ."

"Is cow punching in Tom's job description?" someone from the crowd loudly interrupted.

"No, Royce, but bison punching is," Mr. Orso said, laughing. "Anyway, until I let you know otherwise, please don't let your children go outside to play. Once the bison are out of the playground and a safe distance from the school, I'll let you know, and we'll have a teacher out there to monitor the kids. So now, without further ado, let me introduce the U.F.O. president, Mr. Lyall Griffith."

The crowd applauded as a tall middle-aged man in a gray hoodie sweatshirt rose from the seats and stepped up to the mic.

"That's the guy who's camped across from Jason," Buck said.

"Yeah," Toni said, "Philo helped him move his generator."

"Philo said the guy had a lot of electronics to charge,"

Buck said. "He must have been using it to charge drone batteries."

Lyall Griffith took the mic and, after thanking the school for hosting the event, went over the competition's rules and procedures. There would be two events, first a race and then an obstacle course, each increasingly more difficult for the three different age groups. The race-course would be flown one pilot at a time and flight times recorded.

"We have three excellent judges," Mr. Griffith went on to report. "Mrs. Bowen, Mrs. Hammonds, and Mr. Suits. They are all expert drone pilots, have judged countless competitions, and their decisions are final."

As he said their names, each of the judges stood. All wore gray hoodies.

"I never thought trying to identify someone wearing gray would be so difficult," Buck said.

"Me neither," Toni admitted.

"I'll be the instructor for all classes this morning," Mr. Griffith stated, and he looked at his watch. "So, we have about ten minutes to get where we need to be, and then, let the U.F.O. games begin!"

A roar of applause went up from the crowd. Some people stayed in the bleachers, and others quickly climbed down. Several teens started setting up props for the competition. They each wore blue Gardiner School jerseys with BRUINS written in yellow above an icon of a grizzly. Two of the teens untied ropes at either end of the bleachers and lowered a net that was suspended from the rafters.

"I guess that's to protect those watching," Toni said as she and Buck climbed down and, lifting the bottom of the net, ducked under.

"I guess," Buck stated. "I'll meet you in the cafeteria. I need to pee."

"Okay," Toni said.

When Buck walked toward the restroom, he noticed several teens were gathered in front of the drinking fountain, all wearing gray competitors hoodies. He recognized one of them. It was the boy driving the pickup at the campground—Jason Dekster.

"Get a load of this," Jason said, holding his phone so the others could see. "He looks like a bobblehead."

The others looked at the phone and started laughing. Buck moved closer and looked over one of their shoulders. On the screen, Buck watched himself walking across the Grand Prismatic parking lot and then stop. With a quizzical expression on his face, he started looking all around, first to the left, then to the front, then up, left, right, and back down.

"Jason," one of the kids said, holding his stomach because he was laughing so hard, "you take the best candid videos! They're hilarious!"

So I was right! Buck thought. *It was Jason flying at Grand Prismatic.*

Angry, Buck turned to go into the restroom. He accidently bumped into the laughing kid, making him stumble into Jason.

"Hey, man, watch where you're going," the kid called out to Buck as he went into the restroom.

"Who was that?" Buck heard one of the kids say.

"I don't know. Must be one of the elementary brats who are competing." Buck recognized Jason's voice. "But take a look at this moose I videoed at our campground."

The teens were all gone when Buck came out of the restroom, but Toni was waiting by the cafeteria door.

"Is something the matter?" Toni asked as Buck walked up to her.

"I finally met Jason," Buck said. He wasn't in any mood to explain the anger and humiliation he felt at the group of boys laughing at him in Jason's video. He didn't even feel like saying he had been right all along about who had been flying the drone. Saying nothing more, he walked into the cafeteria, where several chairs were lined up in front of a table filled with drones, batteries, and controllers. Hearing Buck's tone, Toni didn't ask anything more and followed Buck to the chairs. Mr. Griffith stood by the table, a blue plastic trunk nearby.

"Hello," Mr. Griffith said as soon as Buck and Toni were seated. "As you just heard in the gym, my name is Lyall Griffith, but I want you to just call me Lyall. First, I want to know who each of you are, how old you are, and if you have ever flown before."

Mr. Griffith looked at the first person.

"I'm Matt. I'm eight, and I'm going to get a drone if I

have fun flying here."

"I'm Matt's sister, Scarlett. I'm thirteen, and I'm here because my mom didn't want Matt to be by himself."

"My name's Jeff, I'm ten, and I've never flown."

"Me neither," Buck admitted. "I'm Buck, and I'm eleven."

Before he looked at the next person, Mr. Griffith said, "Buck Bray, right? From the TV show?"

All the others looked over at Buck. "Yep, that's me," he said, not really wanting the attention.

"I'm camping at Mammoth, too," Mr. Griffith said. "Philo told me about you and your show." Then he moved on to the next person.

"I'm Toni. My dad is Buck's cameraman. I'm eleven, and I've never flown."

"I'm Lisa. I'm ten. I've tried to fly, but I'm not any good."

"Well, I'm glad you're all taking a class. I hope you enjoy it, and maybe one day, you'll be one of the competitors," Lyall said. "We're going to start with basics about drones, and then we'll all get to try flying one."

Lyall picked up a drone and started telling the names of

all the parts and how they worked.

"It's complex, but quadcopters can fly because of one of the basic laws of physics," Lyall stated. "When there is one force, there will be an opposite but equal force. So, when the rotors spin, the air is forced downward. What do you think the opposite force will be?"

Everyone but Scarlett raised their hands. Lyall called on Matt.

"The drone is forced upward?" Matt said.

"Exactly," Lyall stated. "You get lift."

Lyall went on to explain about the controller, telling how to insert the battery, turn it on, and operate it with the joysticks.

"My friend has a drone, but he flies it using his phone, not a controller," Scarlett said.

"Yes, some drones are flown with phones," Lyall stated. "Let me show you."

Lyall opened the lid on the blue trunk and took out a small drone, turned it on, and put it on the table. Then he pulled a phone from his pocket.

"That's an OR-213," Buck whispered to Toni.

"I just bring up this app," Lyall said, "and, voilà, there are the controls to fly it. Instead of the joysticks on a flight controller, you just use these two little circles on the screen, moving them with your thumbs."

As he spoke, Lyall walked across in the front of the row of participants, showing them the circles on the phone.

"And what's cool," Lyall continued, "is I can watch the video it's taking right on the phone. Come here and watch."

Everyone got up and crowded together, watching as Lyall's thumbs moved the circles. The drone took off and as it flew around the room, they could see the video it was recording. Lyall landed the drone next to the blue trunk.

"So, now it's your turn to fly," he said, putting his phone back in his pocket. "First I want you to try lifting the drone straight up ten feet, and then letting it go straight back down to land. After you have successfully done that a few times, see if you can lift it and make it move in a circle. Each battery lasts seven minutes, so work on just that for the life of one battery."

Everyone selected a drone, loaded the battery, and then went to different areas of the cafeteria. Buck got his drone to lift, but when he tried to land it, it darted off in front of him, nose-dived, and crashed. He tried again and again, each time ending with the same result, and each time he grew more frustrated.

As Buck once again turned his crashed drone right side up, he looked across the room. Toni's drone was moving in a big circle about five feet above the floor, as was Jeff's. Matt's drone was moving wildly in chaotic circles, and, once, his sister had to duck to keep from being hit.

Buck looked over at Lisa. Her drone was upside down on the ground. The rotors were still spinning, and so was the drone—rotating in circles while scooting across the floor.

At least I'm not the worst, Buck thought, but even so, it did not decrease his amount of aggravation. He finally got the drone to lift and move in a circle when the battery died and the rotors stopped. The drone crashed to the cafeteria floor.

All the drones were out of power within seconds of each other.

"Buck and Lisa, you need more practice at lift, circle,

and land," Lyall said as they came up to the table to get another battery. "I want the rest of you to stand on that side of the room and see if you can fly your drones across the room to those cones and back."

With the second battery, Buck kept practicing lifting, circling, and landing. He gradually got better. He glanced over and saw Toni fly her drone across the room and back. With the third battery, Buck had advanced to flying across the room, but most of his attempts ended in crashes. Toni, however, was sending her drone across the room, making it hover above the cone, lift to the ceiling, and then go straight back down in a perfect landing. Then, lifting up again, the drone flew back across the room, hovered, and landed at her feet.

"Bravo!" Lyall yelled out. "I think we've got a future competitor here!"

TAKE 18:

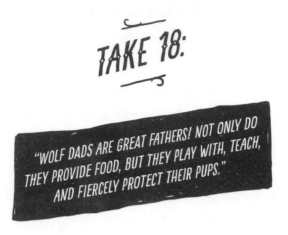

"WOLF DADS ARE GREAT FATHERS! NOT ONLY DO THEY PROVIDE FOOD, BUT THEY PLAY WITH, TEACH, AND FIERCELY PROTECT THEIR PUPS."

After the lesson, Buck and Toni helped Lyall put all the drones and controllers into the blue trunk. Then they headed back to the gym.

"I stunk, but you were really good," Buck said.

"Thanks," said Toni. "You were getting the hang of it, though. A couple more batteries and you would have been right over there, racing with them." Buck looked toward the contestants who sat in chairs lined up against the gym's far wall, their drones in their laps. Kale sat in the third chair.

"Yeah, right," Buck said as the two headed up the bleachers. Kayla was seated in the row behind her parents. Two soda cans saved the spaces beside her.

"Kale got you a soda," Kayla said. "Hope you like root beer."

"Love it," Toni said, picking up a can and sitting down next to Kayla. Buck picked up the other can and sat down next to Toni, just as Mr. Orso walked out to the middle of the gym with a microphone in his hand.

"If I can please have your attention," he said. "The bison are all out of the playground, so it's safe for the kids to go out now, if they'd like. One of our kindergarten teachers is in the lobby. She'll escort the kids out and will remain outside to supervise them."

A few little kids scurried from the bleachers and ran out the gym door. Mr. Orso handed the mic to one of the judges and sat down on the bottom row of the bleachers.

"We'll now proceed to the middle-school division, starting with the seven-lap race," the judge stated. "Contestant number one, please ready your drone for takeoff and take your place at the pilot's box."

A tall girl stood and walked to an X made of red tape on the floor. She set her drone on the X and then stepped into a taped square a few feet away. At the sound of a buzzer, her drone lifted and started flying. It raced around and around the gym, going through a series of hoops set up around the perimeter of the room on stands about ten feet from the floor. She had flown it perfectly for three laps, but on the fourth, the edge of a rotor nicked a hoop. The drone spun out of control, crashed into the net, and dropped to the gym floor. As the judges wrote on their clipboards, the girl walked over to the drone, picked it up, and returned to her seat.

"Good thing there's a net," Buck whispered to Toni as the crowd politely clapped for the girl's attempt.

"Contestant number two, please," the judge said into the mic. The boy in the next chair got up, positioned his drone on the X, and walked to the pilot's square.

"That guy is really good," Kayla whispered to Buck and Toni as the buzzer went off. "I've seen him win at other competitions." They watched the boy race his drone, successfully going through all the hoops.

"Don't they announce how much time it took?" Buck asked as the boy sat down.

"No," Kayla said, "not until the end, but most of the contestants are keeping track of the time they have to beat. And so are a lot of people up here."

Buck looked down at Mrs. Kolson. She had a stopwatch in her hand. Glancing around, he noticed many others either had stopwatches or their phones out in front of them, most likely with a timer app opened up. Buck looked back toward the gym floor as contestant number three was called. Kale placed his drone on the X and stepped into the pilot's square, then the buzzer went off. He flew the drone around and around, not missing a single hoop.

"Darn," Kayla said, looking over at her mother's stopwatch. "Two seconds slower."

"His time was good, though," Mr. Kolson said.

The next three contestants flew. One missed a hoop but didn't crash. The other two both flew perfectly.

"It'll be close. One had the same time as Kale, but my mom's stopwatch only goes to one-tenth of a second,"

Kayla said. "The judges time them to one-hundredth of a second, so we won't know until the awards ceremony."

As the last contestant took her place and started to fly, Buck heard a bunch of snickering behind him and then Jason's voice.

"The third kid from the left," Jason said. Then he quietly said something else that Buck couldn't hear, and the others all snickered again. Buck looked over to see if Toni, Kayla, or her parents had heard Jason, but Toni and Kayla were both talking, and Mr. and Mrs. Kolson were intent on the race.

"I'll be right back," Buck said to Toni. He moved a few rows higher so he could better hear what Jason was saying.

"He's such a little nerd," Jason said. "I thought he was going to cry when I told him I'd smash his drone if he tattled."

"Let me see the video again," one of the kids said, and Jason handed him his phone. "How did you take this? Did you go outside?"

"No, I just opened the window in the teachers' lounge and flew from there," Jason said. "That stupid janitor driving the tractor didn't even know my little OR-213 was out there."

"That bison did, though," the other kid said, laughing. "It doesn't want to go through that gate."

"I kept buzzing past its head every time it looked toward the gate." Jason laughed. "Then that little twerp came in, and I almost lost my drone."

"Did it crash?"

"Yeah, because I turned around to see who came in behind me. The kid started to run back out, but I grabbed hold of his hood," Jason said. "I asked him if he wanted something, and he just said yes, and nothing else."

"So what did you do?" another kid asked.

"I got right in his face and said, 'What are you doing in here, spying on me?'"

"What did he say?" a different kid asked.

"He said, 'Getting sodas, and no,'" Jason said. "It was weird—'Getting sodas, and no.' Who answers a question like that?"

"So what did you do then?" the first kid asked.

"Well, I couldn't let him just leave. He'd probably tell

his parents why he didn't come back with a soda," Jason said. "So I shoved him at the soda machine and told him to get his drink and get out of there. And I said if he tattled, I'd crush his drone."

"Do you think he told his parents?"

"No, his family is right down there." Jason pointed down toward where the Kolsons sat. "They don't look upset, do they?"

"What about your drone?"

"Luckily, it landed upright, but I thought it was going to be smashed. The bison almost stepped on it as it charged out the gate," Jason said. "Then I thought the tractor was going to hit it. My drone was right between the tires as it drove out. But after the janitor was gone, I just flew it back in through the window."

For the second time that morning, Buck was furious. The last contestant had finished her flight, and it was announced there would be a short intermission while the props were rearranged for the obstacle course. Buck saw the principal walk out through the open gym doors. Buck quickly ran down the bleachers and followed him. In the lobby, he saw Mr. Orso enter a small office behind the reception counter.

"Can I talk with you for a second?" Buck called out over the counter.

"Sure," Mr. Orso said. "There's a door just around the corner."

Buck walked around the corner and went through the door, across the back of the reception counter, and into Mr. Orso's office.

"What can I help you with?" Mr. Orso asked.

"I need you to contact somebody for me," Buck said, and he shut the door behind him. Several minutes later, the door opened again.

"You did the right thing," Mr. Orso said. "I'll take care of it. It's a good thing he's not one of our students. He'd have to answer to me, too."

Mr. Orso picked up the phone, and as Buck walked back behind the reception counter toward the door, he heard the man say, "Could you please put me in contact with Isabel Hodges?"

Buck got back to his seat just as the tall girl once again

stepped into the pilot's box.

"Where did you go?" Toni asked him as the girl's drone rose and headed toward the side of the gym where three obstacles were set out. Each had two pillars with a horizontal beam stretched across the top, making a bridge.

"Taking care of business. I'll tell you later," Buck said, and he started watching the competition.

At the first obstacle, the drone went between the two pillars. Then, at the next obstacle, it lifted up and flew over the top. At the third, it flew back between the pillars. The drone then turned and headed toward the middle of the gym, where there were several tall vertical tubes standing in a circle. A space between two of the tubes would allow a drone to enter, but all the other tubes were set too close together. The drone made it into the gap, hovered, and then started rising vertically to the top. When it cleared the top, it sped across the room to a long, wide pipe lying horizontally on the ground. The drone flew into the pipe, but then there was a crashing sound. The drone never came out the other end. The girl walked over to the pipe, got down on her hands and knees, and crawled in. In a couple of seconds, she backed out, holding her drone.

"I feel bad for her," Toni said as the crowd politely clapped for the girl. "That must be awfully embarrassing."

"You need to go back to the baby division," a voice called from the bleachers above them.

Many in the bleachers, including the Kolsons, looked back to see who had called out. Mr. Kolson then turned to his wife and said, "That kid needs to show some manners and good sportsmanship."

As the contestant walked back to her seat, she wiped her sleeve across her eyes and pulled the hood of her sweatshirt over her head.

"That was mean," Toni said to Buck.

"*That* was Jason," Buck said.

When it was Kale's turn, Buck held his breath, hoping that Jason wouldn't yell something out at Kale, too. But as Kale walked to the pilot's square, Mr. Kolson rose, walked up the bleachers, and sat down right behind Jason. He leaned over and said something in Jason's ear. The whole group of teens was extremely quiet as Kale flew the obstacle course. He successfully maneuvered his drone through and over the series of pillar and bridge obstacles, went up the vertical chute, through the tunnel, and then zigzagged back and forth through some hoops set in an alternating pattern. He landed the drone on top of one of the bridges, lifted off again, then finally set the drone down, right on the red X. The crowd applauded, and Kale beamed from ear to ear.

The rest of the middle-school contestants flew the obstacle course, some perfectly, others missing an obstacle, but none crashing. The contestants then made their way across the gym and into the bleachers. Kale sat down next to Kayla. His sister and his parents, as well as Buck and Toni, congratulated him on his performance.

"Thanks," Kale said, but then he leaned over to his father. "Did you talk to him?"

Mr. Kolson shook his head and quietly responded, "We'll take care of it at lunchtime."

Soon, the high-school contestants went to the gym floor. Jason sat in the second chair. As before, the judge called each contestant to the pilot's box, and one by one, each contestant took his or her turn, racing their drone around the room through the hoops.

"Their times were all really close," Mrs. Kolson said as even more obstacles were set up on the gym floor. "I don't know for certain, but I think that second boy was the fastest."

The judge announced that the second event, the obstacle course, would now begin. The first contestant went to the pilot's box. He performed well, but when he was supposed to sharply weave back and forth and up and down through a series of vertical and horizontal poles, he missed one of the turns.

"He'll lose some points on that, but he could still win," Kayla said as the contestant finished the course without any more errors. "It all depends on how everyone else does."

The first contestant headed back to his seat, and the judge called for the second contestant. Jason got up and walked toward the red X. As he passed the other boy, he leaned over and quietly said something to him. The other boy gave Jason a dirty look and kept on walking, but Jason had a smug smile on his face.

"I bet he didn't congratulate him," Buck said to Toni.

"Probably not," Toni said.

Jason turned on his drone, set it on the X, and stepped into the pilot's box. Then he looked at the judges, waiting for them to sound the buzzer. But before they did so, Mr. Orso came jogging into the gym and over to one of the judges. He spoke with the judge for a second. The judge looked at Jason, and then toward the gym doors. Buck looked toward the doors too. There stood Isabel in her ranger's uniform, and next to her was a police officer.

With hushed voices, the people in the bleachers all started talking among themselves. The judge and the principal went over and spoke to Jason. Jason started shaking his head and backing away from them. As he did, the ranger and the policeman hurried across the gym.

Charging down the bleachers toward his son, Jason's father bellowed out, "What's going on?"

Isabel, the policeman, and Mr. Dekster all reached Jason at about the same time. The judge picked up Jason's drone and turned it off as the ranger and the officer spoke with Jason and his father. Many in the bleachers were now straining to hear what was being said, but from across the gym, the conversation could not be heard.

It wasn't long before the police officer, gripping Jason's arm, led the boy across the gym and exited. Jason's father was right behind them. Isabel took the drone from the judge and followed too.

The audience immediately hushed as the judge picked up the microphone.

"I'm sorry for the disruption," the judge said to the contestants. "Will the next contestant please proceed to the pilot's square?"

Then the judge looked toward the other two judges and said, "Jason Dekster has been disqualified."

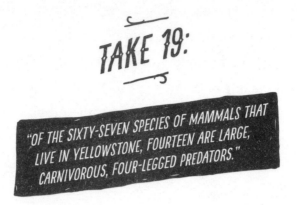

TAKE 19:

"OF THE SIXTY-SEVEN SPECIES OF MAMMALS THAT LIVE IN YELLOWSTONE, FOURTEEN ARE LARGE, CARNIVOROUS, FOUR-LEGGED PREDATORS."

As the next contestant started flying her drone, Toni turned to Buck.

"I know you had something to do with that," she whispered. "What's going on?"

"I'll tell you when we can talk in private," Buck whispered back.

They watched the rest of the competition. Afterward, while everyone filed out of the gym for lunch, Buck turned to the Kolsons.

"Toni and I will meet you in the cafeteria, but I want

her to take my picture by the grizzly statue first," he said. Then he hurried Toni out the school's front door.

"I went to Mr. Orso during intermission to tell him I had proof about Jason flying drones in Yellowstone," Buck stated as soon as they were out of earshot of the others.

"You suspected him," Toni said, "but what proof did you have?"

"Before our class, I saw Jason showing his friends a video he took of me at Grand Prismatic. He also had a video of the moose in the campground," Buck said, "but what's worse is . . ."

"Did he poison Odin?" Toni blurted out.

"I don't know," Buck said, "but if he did, I bet he would have been bragging about it."

"Yeah, probably," Toni agreed.

"Anyway, when I went and sat closer to Jason during the middle-school competition, he was showing his friends a video he took of the bison on the playground," Buck said. "And he told them that he had threatened Kale."

"You're kidding!" Toni gasped.

Buck told Toni everything he had heard. "That's when I decided I wasn't going to wait around. I told Mr. Orso everything, and he called Isabel and the police."

"Why the police?" Toni asked. "Wouldn't the rangers be in charge of stuff going on in the park?"

"When he flew the OR-213 out to the playground, Jason was flying within five miles of an airport," Buck stated.

"Oh yeah," Toni said. "Are you going to tell Mr. and Mrs. Kolson about Jason bullying Kale?"

"Mr. Orso said he'd talk with them," Buck said, "but he asked me not to say anything to anybody."

"You told me," Toni said, grinning.

"Yeah, but you'd pester me until I did," Buck said, smiling back. "Besides, we're in this together."

"Well, that solves who was flying at Grand Prismatic and the campground," Toni said, "but we still don't know who poisoned Odin. Did you tell Mr. Orso about that?"

"No, but I'm sure Isabel will be asking Jason about it," Buck said. He pulled out his camera. "Here, I really do want a picture of me with the grizzly."

Toni quickly snapped a picture, and Buck took one of her, too. When they went back inside, Kayla was sitting by herself on a bench in the lobby.

"My parents are in there with Kale," Kayla said, pointing toward Mr. Orso's closed office door. "Seems Jason was bullying Kale."

"You're kidding?" Toni asked, pretending as if she didn't already know about the situation.

"No," Kayla said. "It makes me so angry when people are mean to him."

The door to Mr. Orso's office opened, and the Kolsons walked out, heading behind the reception counter toward the side door.

"I don't know what else that boy did," Mr. Kolson said to his son, "but you did the right thing telling us how he treated you."

Buck glanced at Toni. Evidently, Mr. Orso had not said anything to the Kolsons about Jason flying drones illegally. As the Kolsons entered the lobby, Buck got up and hurried over to Kale.

"You flew great!" Buck said. "You should have seen me

in class—I kept crashing. How do you do it so well?"

"Thanks," Kale said, his face immediately smiling. "I practice a lot."

The six of them found a place to eat in the cafeteria. Buck sat by Kale and kept asking him questions about flying drones, and Kale readily answered them. Soon lunch was over, and it wasn't long before Kale was standing in the middle of the gym during the awards ceremony, a medal being hung around his neck by Lyall Griffith. Afterward, Kale showed his family and Buck and Toni the medal. A drone was etched into the middle, and written around the top edge were the words UNMANNED FLIGHTS ORGANIZATION COMPETITION. Curved around the bottom edge, it said MIDDLE-SCHOOL DIVISION: SECOND PLACE.

As contestants and their families filed out of the school, Mr. Orso, Lyall Griffith, and the three judges all stood by the front door, saying goodbye.

"Would it be okay if we left our RV parked here while we wander around town a bit?" Mr. Kolson asked Mr. Orso. "My wife wants to get a picture of the Roosevelt Arch and go to some of the gift shops."

"No problem," Mr. Orso said. "And congratulations again, Kale."

"Thanks," responded Mr. Kolson and Kale.

At one of the gift stores, while Toni and Kayla were trying on ball caps and Mr. and Mrs. Kolson were picking out T-shirts, Buck pulled something from a display. He went to the cashier and paid for it.

"It's for Toni," he said to Kale, who stood in line behind him. When Kale finished making his purchase, Buck suggested they wait outside for the others. The two stood leaning against the storefront window. Down the road was a car wash. Several vehicles were lined up waiting to drive in. Buck watched a black pickup with a camper shell over the bed drive out the other side, the sun reflecting off its clean sides. Soon Mr. and Mrs. Kolson joined the boys, followed by Toni and Kayla.

"Do you like our ball caps?" Kayla asked. Both she and Toni were wearing identical olive-green caps embroidered with a howling wolf standing in front of mountains.

"Yes," both Buck and Kale answered at the same time.

"Good," Toni said, "because I got one for you, Kale."

"And I got one for you, too, Buck," Kayla added.

The girls each gave the boys a bag.

"Thanks!" both boys said.

"This is for you," Kale said to his sister. He handed her a small book about animal tracks. Buck dug around in his pocket.

"And I thought you'd like this, Toni," Buck added. He handed Toni a small card. Attached to it was an enameled pin of a gray wolf standing on top of the words YELLOW-STONE NATIONAL PARK.

"Awesome, thanks!" Toni said. She immediately took off her backpack and stuck the pin above the Canyonlands patch, then held the pack up for everyone to see. "Looks good there, doesn't it?"

As the group walked back to the RV, Buck quietly told Toni he had seen a black truck being washed.

"You and your black trucks, Buck," Toni said, shaking her head. Then she started reading aloud information about the wolf restoration program that was written on the back of the pin's card.

"'In 1996, when the wolves were brought back, the

Yellowstone ecosystem once again had all its predators,'" she finished up.

Unfortunately, Buck thought to himself, *another predator has come to the park. And I'm certain he drives a black pickup.*

TAKE 20:

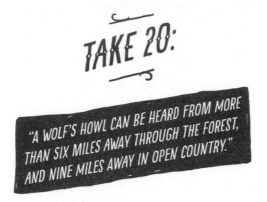

"A WOLF'S HOWL CAN BE HEARD FROM MORE THAN SIX MILES AWAY THROUGH THE FOREST, AND NINE MILES AWAY IN OPEN COUNTRY."

Returning to the campground, Mr. Kolson stopped at Buck and Toni's campsite. As the two kids jumped out, thanking the Kolsons, Dad and Shoop hurried over.

"Why don't you join us for a cookout tonight?" Dad asked. "We've got plenty of hot dogs and baked beans."

"All right!" Buck said. "The Green Beast will smell just like fumaroles tonight!"

"Buck!" Dad scolded. "Don't be crass!"

"A cookout would be wonderful," Mrs. Kolson said, trying not to laugh. "Thank you. We'll bring some fresh veggies."

As the Kolsons pulled away, Buck turned to Dad and Shoop, a serious look now on his face. "You're going to hear about some stuff that went on with a kid named Jason, but there's more to it than what the Kolsons know."

Buck went on to tell the two men about the videos that Jason had filmed and how he had bullied Kale. "I told Mr. Orso, the school principal, and he contacted the authorities."

Both Dad and Shoop nodded. "Good, that was the right thing to do," Dad said. "I'm proud of you, Buck."

"I didn't tell Mr. Orso about Odin," Buck added.

"Don't worry. We won't discuss that tonight either," Dad stated.

"Can we invite Philo tonight too?" Toni asked.

"Sure," Dad said. "Run on up there and do that."

As Buck and Toni headed up the road, a black pickup headed slowly toward them. Both kids immediately stepped to the side of the road and stopped walking.

"Is that Jason?" Toni asked with alarm. Buck squinted, focusing on the approaching license plate.

"No," he said, letting out a sigh of relief. The pickup slowed to a stop beside the kids, and Lyall Griffith rolled down his window.

"Hey! My ace student!" Lyall said. "And my most-improved student, too."

Both of the kids smiled, but Buck could feel his face turning red with embarrassment, knowing how poorly he had flown.

"Don't worry," Lyall said, grinning at Buck. "I won't put it out on social media."

"Good," said Buck, smiling back. "We're having a cookout tonight. The Kolsons are coming, and we're inviting Philo. I'm sure my dad won't mind if you join us too."

"That sounds great," Lyall said. "I'll be there."

"We're in number twenty-two," Toni said as he started to drive away.

"I knew that," Lyall called back. "Everybody in this campground has noticed that weird green camper of yours!"

When Buck and Toni reached Philo's, Philo was taking

down the sign that said BUT NOT NOW! His golf cart was parked nearby, a rake, bucket, and scrub brush in the back.

"Howdy," Philo said.

"We want to invite you to our cookout," Toni said.

"The Kolsons are coming, and so is Lyall Griffith," Buck added.

"Hot diggity dog! I'll bring some extra firewood," Philo said. He hung the BUT NOT NOW! sign back up and got into the golf cart. "Hop in."

Philo drove over to the shed. As he put away the cleaning supplies, Buck and Toni each took a bundle of wood from a stack next to the shed and put them in the back of the cart. Philo then drove to the Bray campsite, where they soon had a blazing fire going. A half hour later, the Kolsons and Lyall joined them, and they sat around the fire, roasting hot dogs and talking about the day's happenings.

"He must have done something besides bullying Kale," Mrs. Kolson said, "for the authorities to get involved."

"Do you think it had anything to do with the drone

you saw at Grand Prismatic?" Kayla asked Buck.

Buck shrugged but didn't say anything. Instead he took a big bite from his hot dog, trying to avoid telling his role in what had happened at the school. He was relieved when, before he could swallow, a ranger's SUV pulled in behind the golf cart, distracting everyone from the subject. When Isabel and Lobo jumped out, Buck introduced them to the Kolsons and Lyall.

"You're just in time for dinner," Dad said. "We've got plenty."

"Thanks!" Lobo said, walking over to the picnic table. "Don't mind if I do."

"We stopped by to fill you in about today," Isabel stated as Lobo put two hot dogs on a metal roasting stick. "And to thank Buck. We confiscated the video from Jason's drone, proving he flew drones here in the park as well as outside the school."

"You knew all along why he was arrested?" Kayla asked Buck.

"Yes, I saw Jason showing kids the videos," Buck confessed, "so I told Mr. Orso. He called the authorities but asked me to keep quiet about it."

"What will happen to him?" Toni asked.

"Jason's being charged with several things," Isabel said. "Flying a drone in the park and harassing animals with a drone—the bison and moose you saw in the videos, Buck—and also a bull elk near the Albright Visitor Center in Mammoth."

"I didn't see that video," Buck stated.

"He'll also face federal charges for flying in a restricted zone," Lobo added, putting the hot dogs on buns and handing one to Isabel.

"Will he go to jail?" Toni asked.

"He might have to go to juvenile detention," Isabel stated, "and will probably have to pay a big fine. But I can guarantee he will be banned from national parks for at least five years."

"Are the Deksters still camping here?" Buck asked.

"No, Lobo and I escorted them out of the park," Isabel stated. "We just got back from following them to Gardiner."

"I had just finished cleaning up their campsite when

you guys came to invite me for dinner," Philo added.

"It's upsetting that someone from the competition was not obeying the laws," Lyall stated. "It gives drone flying a bad reputation."

"It's not bad," Kale said quietly.

"No, it's not," Lyall said, "if you're flying responsibly."

"And flying drones even helps people," Kayla added. "Like bringing people medicine."

"Kale," Mrs. Kolson said, "tell everyone what you read last week."

"Someone used a quadcopter to drop life jackets to two people who were being pulled out to sea by a riptide," Kale answered. "It kept them from drowning before a boat could rescue them."

"Wow!" Buck said. "If I were drowning, I'd hope someone was better at flying a drone than I was!"

Everyone chuckled.

"You just need practice," Lyall said, then he turned to Shoop. "You should get one. You'd get some great aerial footage for your TV show."

"I might have to think about that," Shoop stated. "I

couldn't use it in the national parks, but maybe other places."

"You should take one of Lyall's classes tomorrow during the adult competition," Buck said. "I'll go with you. I could use another class."

"Sorry," Lyall said. "There aren't any classes tomorrow. Just the adult competition. And I won't even be at that. I've got other plans."

"I could teach you," Kale said quietly to Shoop.

"We won't have time, Kale," Mr. Kolson said. "We have to leave tomorrow. But I was thinking, if we got going early, we'd go see if we could spot the wolves at Slough Creek before we left."

"Thanks for offering, though," Shoop said to the boy. "That was really nice."

"I hate to disappoint you," Lobo said to the Kolsons, "but the Slough Creek Road has been temporarily closed. You won't be able to get in there."

"Why?" Kayla asked. Buck glanced at Lobo, wondering if he was going to tell them what was going on.

"The wolves have been a little stressed lately," Lobo

answered, glancing back at Buck. "We're just letting them have some time to themselves without spotters around."

"Well, that's too bad, but our vacation isn't over yet," Mrs. Kolson said cheerily. "I brought the makings for s'mores."

"All right!" the four kids said, and jumped up, grabbing the roasting sticks.

"Oh man," Buck suddenly said as he put his marshmallow over the flames. "We never hiked into town to get ice cream cones. Toni owes me one, and Kayla owes Kale one too. Chocolate, right, Kale?"

"Right," Kale replied.

"What time does the general store open?" Kayla asked Philo.

"Nine," Philo answered.

"Since we don't have to get up early to wolf watch, maybe we kids could go in the morning while you pack up," Kayla suggested to her parents. "And you could pick us up in town and bring Buck and Toni back here before we head out."

"Checkout isn't until ten, and it only takes about a half

hour to hike to town," Philo said. "They'd have plenty of time."

"Ice cream at nine in the morning?" Mrs. Kolson said.

"I don't think it would hurt them just this one time," Mr. Kolson said, winking at the kids.

"I guess," Mrs. Kolson said, "if it's all right with Dan and Shoop."

"Fine with me," Dad said.

"Me too," Shoop said.

"Super," Kayla said, giving the other kids a thumbs-up.

The evening grew dark. Stars filled the sky, and the flames turned to pulsing red embers in the circle of the fire ring. They watched the fire, now talking in the hushed tones that darkness seemed to require. Suddenly a low, lonely howl split the night's quiet, coming from the mountains that rose above the Gardner River. Its pitch rose up high, held the note, and then slowly lowered in tone before becoming silent. But only for half a second. Another howl soon rose up again, long and clear.

"Is that a wolf?" Buck whispered.

"The Gardner pack," Lobo said quietly. "It's a good-size

pack. Thirteen adults and five pups. Their den isn't too far from here—just across the river on the other side of those cliffs."

As he spoke, another wolf started howling, and then another and another. Soon the night was filled with a chorus of long, resonant sounds moving up and down the scales and echoing through the mountains. The group sat by the fire, mesmerized by the wolves' serenade. Only Shoop spoke.

"That's the most beautiful sound I've ever heard," he said quietly.

TAKE 21:

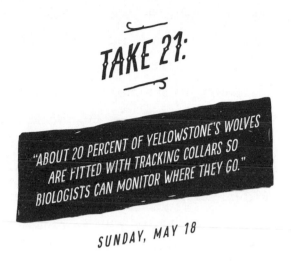

"ABOUT 20 PERCENT OF YELLOWSTONE'S WOLVES ARE FITTED WITH TRACKING COLLARS SO BIOLOGISTS CAN MONITOR WHERE THEY GO."

SUNDAY, MAY 18

At eight thirty the next morning, Buck, Toni, Kayla, and Kale, each wearing their new ball caps, met at the amphitheater and headed up the trail. When they reached the bench, they stopped. Raising his binoculars, Buck looked over the campground. Mr. Kolson was below them, folding up camp chairs and putting them in the RV's storage area. A pickup with a camper in the truck bed was driving around the bend onto the upper tier. It kept going until it reached the last site, and then it backed into where Jason Dekster and his father had previously camped. Across the road, the young couple was sitting in camp chairs, the toddler in the woman's lap. And at the site next to theirs, Lyall Griffith was sitting at his picnic table. Down at the campground entrance, a red pickup with a long camper trailer and two SEE AMERICA FIRST RVs were already lined up at the registration area. Philo was walking from the window of the second vehicle toward the third when a fourth camper pulled in. Buck followed the campground road with his binoculars until he reached the Green Beast.

"Wow!" he exclaimed. "A bull moose is walking toward our camper!"

A huge, long-legged creature with massive antlers walked right between the camper and the picnic table. It stopped for a moment and then went right up to the kitchen window and looked in.

"I wish I was in there right now," Buck said. He handed the binoculars to Kale, who then shared them with his sister, and then finally Toni. The entire time, the moose stood at the side of the camper, looking in.

"Maybe it sees its reflection in the glass," Toni said,

handing the binoculars back to Buck. "I wonder if Shoop is in there filming it."

"More than likely," Buck said. They continued to pass the binoculars around until the moose finally turned away. In just a few steps, it walked to the main road, crossed it, and went up the hill with the railroad tie steps. Soon, it disappeared over the top. The four kids then headed on up their trail, alert to the possibility that they could come upon wildlife around any bend.

Although the trail went uphill, it wound back and forth enough that, until the last several yards, it wasn't terribly steep. The last few yards, however, went almost straight up, and suddenly they were at the top, standing beside the road at the edge of town. They hurried down the sidewalk to the Mammoth General Store. The manager was just unlocking the doors.

"You're here bright and early," she stated.

"We want to get ice cream cones," Kayla said.

"I'm sorry," the woman replied. "The fountain doesn't open until eleven."

"Darn," Buck said. "Their parents are checking out of

the campground and will pick us all up just after ten."

The kids turned to leave, but the manager stopped them.

"Wait a second," she said, a grin on her face. "Where are you from?"

At the same time, Kayla and Kale responded Oregon, while Toni said Missouri, and Buck stated Indiana.

"Well, I believe it is just now eleven o'clock in Indiana," the woman said. "Just don't tell anyone our hours are based on people's home time zones."

"Thanks!" the four kids said.

They followed the woman to the back of the store, where tubs of colorful ice cream sat in a freezer behind a glass shield. A sign on the wall listed the flavor names.

"Don't you have any chocolate?" Buck asked.

"Sure. Mud Pots is chocolate," the woman said. Then she rapidly rattled off a description of the flavors listed on the sign. "Grand Prismatic is rainbow sherbet, Elk Drops is vanilla with chocolate-covered peanuts. Moose Antlers has caramel swirls and sliced almonds. Huckle-Beary is just like it sounds—huckleberry—it tastes like blueberries.

Geyser Gusher tastes like grape bubble gum, and Old Faithful is just plain old vanilla."

"Wow," Buck said, "you have that memorized well!"

"I either say it or hear it a gazillion times a day," the woman said with a laugh. "I could repeat it in my sleep."

"Believe me, I understand how that is," Buck said. "I'll have one scoop of Mud Pots and one of Elk Drops, please, and she's paying for it." Buck motioned toward Toni.

"And I'll have a scoop of Huckle-Beary and Geyser Gusher, please," Toni said.

"Geyser Gusher?" Buck said, wrinkling his nose. "That sounds gross."

"I like grape bubble gum," Toni replied.

"I don't," Kayla said. "I'll take two scoops of Grand Prismatic, please. And I'm paying for his." She pointed to her brother.

"What would you like?" the woman asked Kale.

"Mud Pots and Moose Antlers, please," Kale answered.

"Nobody ever gets Old Faithful," the woman said as she scooped out the ice cream. "That tub will probably still be there at the end of the summer."

Thanking the woman once again, Toni and Kayla paid for the cones. Outside, the four kids carried them across the road to the grassy park where some picnic tables were.

"There were a bunch of elk in here the other day," Buck told the Kolsons.

"There's one over there now," Kayla said. "A big bull by the Albright Visitor Center."

"It must be the one Jason videoed," Toni said. "We saw it the other day, too. That must be its favorite spot."

The four sat side by side on a picnic table with their feet on the bench and their backs to the road, eating their ice cream cones while watching people stop to take pictures of the bull elk. They had just finished their last bites when they heard Mr. Kolson's voice calling the twins' names. Turning around, they saw the RV stopped in the road. Several cars were lining up behind him, and one of them honked.

"There's no place to park here," Mr. Kolson quickly said. "I'm going to drive around the block and come back the opposite direction. Be waiting right there at the curb, ready to hop in."

As the RV continued up the road, the four kids went over to the curb. Soon, the RV returned, stopping briefly to pick them up.

"Why are you so early?" Kayla asked as the kids all sat down at the table. "It's only nine thirty."

"It didn't take long to pack up," Mrs. Kolson said, "so we thought we'd get some ice cream, too."

"But we didn't see a long-enough parking spot," Mr. Kolson said.

"The ice cream fountain doesn't open until eleven, anyway," Kayla said.

"Oh," Mrs. Kolson said. "That's too bad. If we can find a parking space, we could wait around until eleven."

"Thanks," Buck said, "but we already had ice cream. It's after eleven in Indiana."

Laughing, the kids explained about the store manager's comment and how she went ahead and sold them cones. By the time they had finished the story, the RV was heading down the hill toward the campground entrance. A line of campers and RVs was clogging the entrance, and more were lining up on the shoulders on both sides of the road.

Mr. Kolson pulled off onto the shoulder behind the last camper.

"Do you mind if I just let you off here?" he asked. "With all these vehicles blocking the way, it would take forever before I could pull in there."

"No problem," Buck said, "it's not a far walk."

"Just a second," Toni said, opening her backpack and pulling out her sketchpad. "I want to get your e-mail address, Kayla." The two girls exchanged addresses. Then, saying goodbye, Buck and Toni jumped out of the RV.

"Be careful crossing the road," Mrs. Kolson said through the open window.

"We'll watch your show!" Kayla called out, too.

The RV pulled back onto the road, heading toward Gardiner. Buck and Toni walked in the grass along the edge of the shoulder, passing camper after camper. When they reached the front of the line, instead of crossing the road to the entrance, Buck stopped.

"Let's climb that hill with the steps that go to the top," he said. "Philo said there was a great view from up there."

"Shouldn't we let our dads know we're back first?"

Toni asked.

"If they're outside, they'll see where we are," Buck said. "It's in plain view of our campsite."

"And if they're not outside?" Toni said.

"Then we'll tell them when we get back," Buck said. "It can't take more than ten minutes to climb up there."

"Okay," Toni said.

They continued on until they reached the beginning of the trail. They could see the Green Beast farther down and across the road.

"I don't see them. They must be inside," Toni said.

"Stop worrying," Buck said, and he headed up the trail.

Just like he had said, it didn't take long to reach the top, and just like Philo had told them, the view was amazing. To the east, tall cliffs rose hundreds of feet above the Gardner River. Even bigger mountains could be seen down the canyon to the north. The path they used to get to the top continued on, leading southeastwardly down the other side of the hill to a group of houses by the rushing river. Beyond the rooftops, the valley stretched upward to more mountains, many still snowcapped. Buck pulled out his camera and took pictures in all different directions.

"It really is pretty up here," Toni said, "but we better head back."

"Okay," Buck agreed. Toni started down the hill, but as Buck took one last picture, a movement caught his eye. He quickly put his binoculars to his eyes and looked at the edge of the cliffs.

"Toni!" Buck cried out. "There's a GERUMAC!"

TAKE 22:

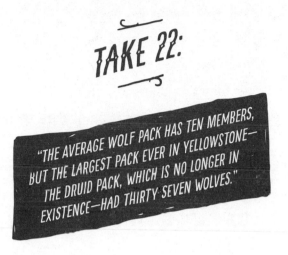

"THE AVERAGE WOLF PACK HAS TEN MEMBERS, BUT THE LARGEST PACK EVER IN YELLOWSTONE— THE DRUID PACK, WHICH IS NO LONGER IN EXISTENCE—HAD THIRTY-SEVEN WOLVES."

Toni ran back up the hill to where Buck stood, his binoculars to his eyes.

"Where?" she asked.

"It came from over those cliffs and is heading toward that other hill where the hiking trailhead sign is," Buck said.

"There's a truck down there at the pullout, but I don't see any people," Toni said.

"It's a black truck with a camper shell," Buck said.

"I know," Toni admitted. "They're kind of like the gray

U.F.O. sweatshirts—they're everywhere."

"Darn! The drone went behind the hill," Buck said. "I can't see it anymore."

"Maybe the pilot's on that trail," Toni said.

Buck scanned the area with his binoculars, going from the pullout to the trailhead sign, and then following the trail toward the river.

"I see three people, but they're not flying anything," Buck said. "They're backpackers, and they're going back toward that truck."

"Maybe the pilot saw them and landed the drone real quick, not wanting the backpackers to see it," Toni suggested.

"Wait a second—I see it again!" Buck called out excitedly. "It's coming this way! It's following the river!"

With the binoculars, he could clearly see the spinning rotors above each of its four charcoal-colored arms.

"There's nothing in the cargo claw," Buck stated. "I hope it didn't drop any kibble near the Gardner pack."

"It could be just another person illegally flying around, taking videos," Toni said.

"Maybe, but I have a feeling that it's the same drone that Kale spotted in Shoop's video," Buck said. "There can't be that many GERUMACs just flying around illegally in Yellowstone. Here, take a look." Buck handed Toni the binoculars.

"I can't locate it," Toni said.

"Find the spruce that's hanging out of the side of the cliff and then scan at that height upstream."

"I found it. No one would see it without binoculars—it just blends in with the rocks," Toni said, watching the GERUMAC as it hugged the side of the cliff. "And the river's noise would have kept those backpackers from hearing it. Maybe the pilot is in the village. It's heading that way."

Buck looked down toward the houses. "I wish we had two sets of binoculars."

"Holy cow!" Toni called out. "It's turning. It's coming straight toward us!"

It wasn't long before Buck could see the drone with his naked eye, and as it approached them, Toni put the binoculars down and looked with her bare eyes too. The

GERUMAC rose as it approached the hill. It was about thirty feet out and thirty feet above their heads when it stopped moving forward and hovered in the air, the camera lens aimed at the two kids.

"Whoever is flying is watching us!" Buck exclaimed. He whipped out his camera and took a picture of it. Instantly the drone sped away, heading toward the campground. Buck and Toni turned to watch it, but as the drone got farther away, it became harder to see. Toni put the binoculars to her eyes again and followed it.

"It crossed the road and is heading toward the upper tier. I think it's going to land," Toni said. "No—wait a second—it's going past the upper tier above the woods beyond the campground and is turning toward the amphitheater. Darn! It's gone behind some trees."

"Can you see anyone on the bench?" Buck asked. "Maybe someone is flying it from there."

"No, but there are plenty of bushes to hide behind. I doubt the pilot would stay in plain sight," Toni answered. She handed the binoculars back to Buck.

"If he's up there, he either got there from the

campground or from Mammoth," Buck said, looping the binoculars' strap around his neck. "Let's go to the amphitheater and see if someone comes down the trail to the campground!"

Buck started for the steps, but Toni hesitated.

"Shouldn't we call Lobo?" Toni asked. "Let him know—"

"No, we need to find out whether the guy is going down to the campground or up to Mammoth," Buck interrupted, "so Lobo will know where to go."

"You're right," Toni said, and the two took off. As they charged down the steps, they could see a steady stream of campers leaving the campground. One by one, those waiting on the shoulder of the road were pulling into the entrance.

"Must be ten o'clock," Buck called out. "Everyone's leaving, and new campers are going in."

"Philo said Sunday mornings are always busy," Toni called back.

They reached the bottom of the steps, ran across the main road, and entered the campground. Instead of turning to go along the lower tier, Buck and Toni continued straight up the hill to the upper tier. The hill was steep, and halfway up they were breathing hard. They stopped running but hurried on.

When they reached the top and turned onto the upper tier, they saw a red pickup pull into Lyall's campsite. It stopped when it was inches from the front bumper of Lyall's truck. A long trailer attached to the red pickup completely blocked the road. The trailer looked brand-new. The driver started moving the pickup back and forth, turning its wheels this way and that way as he tried to maneuver the trailer into the site across the road from Lyall's site. Buck and Toni kept on going, passing the little redheaded boy who was playing in the dirt of the first campsite. His mother sat reading in a camp chair nearby.

"She doesn't look like she's noticed a drone," Toni whispered to Buck.

"Maybe she's like you and doesn't notice anything when she's reading," Buck whispered back.

"Unlike you, I have good concentration skills," Toni said. They continued on, watching the pickup trying to get the trailer backed into the driveway. The rig was still blocking the road, and the driver didn't even seem to be aware that Buck and Toni were approaching. His head was turned away from the kids as he looked into his side-view mirror.

"That guy sure can't back a trailer," Buck said.

"He needs a pull-through site like we have, not a back-in site," Toni said.

"Let's cut through Lyall's campsite."

"Good idea. Maybe he saw the drone fly over."

The two stepped off the road and started winding through the sagebrush and bushes that separated Lyall's campsite from the young couple's. They headed toward Lyall's pickup, which was backed into the site's driveway. As they approached the side of the truck, their faces were reflected in the shell's dark-tinted window.

"Our ball caps look good, don't they?" Toni said.

"Yeah," Buck stated. "It's amazing. You can't see through any of the windows, even this close."

Toni headed toward the back of the truck, but Buck walked up to its side. Putting his hands on either side of his head, he put his face right up to the window.

"Buck!" Toni said, stopping and looking over at him. "What are you doing?"

"I just wanted to know if you could see in at all, but the only way is if you stick your face right up to the window. All that's in there are a generator and that blue trunk he kept the drones in."

"I know," Toni said. "I can see that from back here. Come on."

Buck came around to the back of the truck. The tailgate was closed, but the shell's door was raised open. Buck stopped again, looking in over the tailgate.

"Buck!" Toni exclaimed. "You're so nosy!"

"I'm just looking," Buck said. "Whatever is on the windows only blocks you from seeing in. From inside looking out, it's just a little darker—like you're looking through sunglasses. Except the front window. It's just clear glass between the truck bed and the cab. But all the other cab windows are tinted."

"Whatever," Toni said. Then as she continued into the main part of the campsite, she called out, "Lyall, are you here?"

There was no answer, and Lyall was not in sight.

Beyond the truck, on the opposite side of the campsite, a tent was set up. Its outside flap was rolled back, and through the zipped-up inner mosquito netting, she could see the tent contained nothing but an empty sleeping bag.

"I guess not," Toni answered her own question. "Come on, Buck."

Toni headed toward the road, passing between Lyall's truck and the campsite's picnic table. The red pickup was no longer in Lyall's driveway but was now in the middle of the road, still blocking it from one side to the other. The trailer was angled sharply from the truck, aimed toward the other campsite driveway. Concentrating on the side-view mirror, the driver slowly moved the truck backward.

"Wait," Buck called out. Toni stopped and turned around again.

"Now what?" she asked impatiently. "If we don't get up to the amphitheater, the guy will leave before we see him."

"My boot's untied," Buck said.

Toni waited as Buck sat down on the picnic table's bench. He leaned over and started to reach for his boot lace but stopped.

"Holy cow!" he cried out. "Look!"

Toni sighed in exasperation but hurried back to him. Buck pointed to the ground near his foot. In the dust was a perfect boot print with five circles lined up in an arc near the ball of the foot, three more on the heel, and zigzag lines everywhere else.

"I can't believe it!" Toni exclaimed, squatting down to examine it.

"Me neither!" Buck said, still leaning over. "The boot prints at Slough Creek were Lyall's!"

"Forget the amphitheater," Toni said. "We need to call Lobo!"

"Just a second—I still need to tie my boot."

As he reached for his lace again, a voice called out. Buck and Toni froze.

"Would you like me to guide you?" The kids heard Lyall's voice coming from the campground road.

"Sure, thanks," another man's voice called out. "This

trailer isn't the easiest thing to maneuver."

"No, I'm sure it's not," Lyall responded. "How long is it, anyway?"

"Thirty-six feet," the driver answered. "Those trailer salesmen sure don't tell you that most campsites aren't made for these things. The driveways are way too short."

"That's why I still tent it," Lyall stated, his voice continually getting closer. "I can go anywhere, but a soft bed would be nice instead of sleeping on the ground."

"Don't stand up," Buck whispered as the two men conversed. "I don't think Lyall has seen us."

"He's standing right next to the red truck," Toni whispered, looking under the picnic table toward the road. "And he's not looking this way. If we keep down, I think we can get behind Lyall's pickup without him noticing. Then we can sneak away."

Keeping low, they scurried to the back of the truck. They had just gotten behind it when they heard Lyall again.

"Let me put this up first, and we'll get that baby in there," he said.

Buck peeked over the tailgate, looking across the truck bed and through the cab's windshield. Lyall was coming into the campsite.

"Hide!" Buck whispered emphatically. He quickly scrambled over the tailgate. The generator was at the back of the truck, pushed to one side. It was tight, but Buck had enough room to squeeze to the right of it. The blue trunk, which was under the shell's window, blocked his way, but he didn't slow down. He quickly climbed over the trunk and sat down behind the generator. Toni followed right behind him.

"I don't think he saw us," she whispered as she sat down next to Buck.

"He can't unless he opens a cab door," Buck whispered, "or comes around back."

The two watched as Lyall walked up to and stopped beside the picnic table. Two black straps looped over the front of his shoulders. He pulled his arm from one of the straps and swung a black pack onto the table. Printed across it in big gray letters was the word *GERUMAC*.

Lyall put his hand in his pocket, pulled out a set of

keys, and pushed a button on one. There was a quick snapping sound as the truck's doors unlocked. Then Lyall picked up the GERUMAC's pack by one of its straps and turned toward the truck.

"Get down," Buck whispered. He slumped behind the generator, resting his head on the curve of the wheel well. Toni quickly slipped off her backpack and ducked down too. The two could no longer see Lyall, but within seconds sunlight filled the cab. Immediately afterward, they heard the passenger door slam shut, and the cab darkened. A quick beep of the horn indicated the doors had been locked again. Then Lyall's head went past the shell's window.

"He's coming toward the back!" Toni whispered. Buck and Toni held their breaths as the sound of footsteps came around the back. Seconds later the shell's door squeaked as it shut and there was a quiet click.

"Don't go any farther—you're just about to jackknife," Lyall called out loudly as he walked past the shell's window toward the road. He continued talking, his voice getting farther away. "You'll need to pull forward and get it straightened out."

"I thought for sure he was going to see us," Buck said quietly.

"Me too. Let's get out of here."

Buck scrambled over the trunk and into the space by the generator. Grabbing the inside handle of the shell's door, he tried to twist it, but it wouldn't budge.

"Oh no!" he said. "He locked it!"

"Are you sure?"

"Of course I'm sure," Buck said. "Do any of the windows open?"

Toni glanced at all three windows. "No. They're just solid pieces of glass, nothing to slide and no cranks."

Buck climbed back across the trunk and went over and looked into the cab.

"He put the GERUMAC in the front seat," he said, then he looked outside. "He must be in back of that trailer. I can't see him anymore."

"What do you think we should do, Buck?"

"I don't know." Buck sat down on the trunk and looked out the side window. "If he leaves again, we can yell. That woman with the little kid would probably hear us, and she could go get help."

"We could be in here forever waiting for him to leave," Toni said.

"There's a big boulder you probably can't see back here." They heard Lyall holler to the driver. "Angle a bit to the right and then come straight back."

"When we first heard Lyall, we should have just said hello and pretended we didn't suspect a thing," Toni said. "But it's too late for that now."

"I'm sorry," Buck said. "When he headed this way, I panicked."

"We both did," Toni said. "It's not your fault. I'm the one who said to hide behind his truck."

"Yeah, but I'm the one who climbed in. We should have just run."

"Well, let's not worry about that now," Toni said. "We need to think of a plan."

"Come back just a foot more," Lyall hollered again. "There, that's good."

Buck watched as Lyall walked toward the front of the

red truck. The driver got out, and the two men talked for a few seconds, then shook hands.

"He's coming back," Buck said as Lyall headed across the road. "But he's going toward his bear box."

Toni got up and sat next to Buck. They watched Lyall open a padlock on the brown metal box and swing one of the doors open.

"There's a cooler in there, and it looks like something on top of it, but I can't tell what it is. Can you?" Buck asked.

"No, he's blocking my view," Toni answered as Lyall leaned over and reached in. The man pulled something out and put it on the bear box. Toni gasped. "Oh my gosh! Do you see what he has?"

On top of the bear box was a bag of dog food.

"I bet he's planning to drop another bunch of kibble!" Buck exclaimed, watching the man add a box of tissues and a pair of yellow rubber gloves to the top of the bear box.

"We need to let Lyall know we're back here," Toni said. "And when he opens up the door, we can run."

"No," Buck said as Lyall snapped the lock shut. "If we did that, Lyall could be out of here before we could get back to the Green Beast. Nobody would know where he went."

"Are you crazy?" Toni said, watching the man stick the gloves into the back pocket of his jeans. "You think we should stay in here?"

"Listen, Toni," Buck said as Lyall picked up the kibble and tissues and turned toward the truck. "If he goes back toward the amphitheater, then we'll make a bunch of noise. Someone will come and get help, and we'll be able to tell Lobo where Lyall is."

"And what if he drives away?" Toni said. "What then? Nobody will know where we are!"

"No, but we'll know where Lyall is," Buck said. "And maybe we can stop him from poisoning any more wolves."

Lyall started whistling as he walked across his campsite. When he reached the picnic table, he set the items down and pulled his keys from his pocket. Buck and Toni quietly moved back behind the generator again. There was the click of the doors unlocking, and soon the sound of whistling moved toward the truck. Buck looked at Toni.

"We've got to decide right now," he said urgently as sunlight suddenly filled the cab. Then the passenger side door slammed shut, and the cab instantly dimmed. The whistling moved around to the front of the truck. Once more, the cab filled with sunlight.

"He's getting in," Buck said. "What do you want to do, Toni?"

The driver's-side door shut. Although he and Toni were both looking toward the cab, from their position neither could see even a bit of Lyall's head.

"You know what I think, but I'll go with whatever you say," Toni said.

"Then we're going with him," Buck said as the truck's engine started.

TAKE 23:

"WITH ITS EYES ON THE FRONT OF ITS HEAD, A WOLF HAS ALMOST A 180-DEGREE FIELD OF VISION. AN ELK'S EYES ARE MORE ON THE SIDES OF ITS HEAD, ALLOWING IT TO SEE 300 DEGREES AND MAKING IT EASIER TO SPOT PREDATORS SNEAKING UP FROM BEHIND. HOWEVER, THE ELK'S VISION IS POOR, AND IT CAN'T FOCUS WELL UNTIL THINGS ARE VERY CLOSE."

Lyall's pickup slowly pulled out of the campsite driveway and turned. Soon, it turned again. The two kids stayed in the same position, keeping down so they wouldn't be seen through the truck's rear window. Through the shell's side window they watched the needled branches of the conifers and the leaves of quaking aspen go by as they rode toward the campground entrance. Then the truck stopped. When it started moving again, it turned right.

"We're heading to Mammoth," Buck stated.

Toni pushed her backpack up under her head. It wasn't

long before they saw buildings as they passed through town. Soon the layers of white limestone deposits at the Mammoth Hot Springs Terraces appeared in the window.

"I wonder where he's going," Toni said.

"I don't know," Buck said. "But I know he's not going back to poison the rest of the Slough Creek pack. He would have turned before the terraces."

"What do you think we should do when he stops?" Toni said. Now, once again, all they could see out the window were trees. "We need to have a plan."

"It's hard to plan when we don't know where we're going," Buck said. "But the main thing is, we have to stop him from flying that drone."

"Yeah, I know," Toni agreed. "I guess we'll just have to figure it out when we get there, wherever that is."

Buck slipped the binoculars strap over his head. "Will you put these in your backpack? They won't do me much good in here."

"Sure," Toni said. She pulled the pack out from under her head, unzipped it, and put in the binoculars. "Hey, I forgot! I have a map in here! Maybe we can use it to help figure out where we're going."

"Super," Buck said. "We can't look out the front without Lyall seeing us. But if we sit with our heads against the front of the truck bed, I can look out the shell's side window. From that angle, I should be able to see the signs for those driving the opposite direction and figure out what we just passed."

"Okay," Toni said. "Don't forget to keep your head down."

Toni moved to the center of the truck, leaving room for Buck on the driver's side. She turned on her side, leaning on her elbow and propping up her head. Buck lay on his back, his neck bent awkwardly.

"You can use my backpack to rest your head on," she said as she spread the map out between them. "It'd probably be more comfortable."

"Thanks," he said, positioning the pack under his neck. "That's a lot better."

"Can you see anything?" Toni asked.

"Just trees," Buck said.

As the truck continued on, Buck kept his eyes to the

window. Toni studied the map.

"Perfect," Buck finally said. "I could see a speed limit sign without any problem. Forty-five miles per hour."

"Good," Toni said. "Let me know when you see a sign that will tell us where we are."

It wasn't long before Buck said, "Sheepeater Cliff. We just passed a sign saying it's a quarter of a mile ahead. So we passed that a quarter of a mile ago. Is it on the map?"

Toni looked at the map. "Right here," she said.

Buck glanced over at the map, and Toni pointed out where they were. Then Buck went back to looking out the window.

"It's about fifteen miles until we get to the first major intersection. That's a third of forty-five, which is how fast we're probably going," Toni said, then continued figuring her math problem aloud. "And a third of an hour—we'll be at that intersection in about twenty minutes."

Suddenly the truck slowed to almost a stop.

"I don't know why he's slowing down here," Toni said. "There aren't any roads to turn onto in this area."

"That's why," Buck said, and pointed to the window.

The huge head of a bull bison went past. "We're in another bison jam!"

They watched as more bison continued walking past both windows. Then the truck started accelerating again.

"That was cool," Toni said. "Too bad we couldn't sit up to see them better."

"Yeah," Buck agreed, continuing to look out the window. Most of the time, he saw only the tops of trees, but every once in a while, his view changed to bright blue sky as they drove past meadows before going back into forests again. He read off several more signs before stating, "We just passed a sign saying Norris Campground."

"We're coming up to the intersection, then," Toni said. She had barely finished speaking when the truck slowed down and stopped, then started up again.

"Guess we're not heading toward Yellowstone Falls," Toni said when the truck didn't turn. "I wonder why we stopped."

"There was a stop sign," Buck said. "I just saw one for cars going the other direction."

"Artists' Paintpots should be next," Toni stated.

A few minutes later, Buck reported, "Artists' Paintpots, a quarter of a mile back." Soon afterward, they drove through clouds of steam, and only gray could be seen from the window.

"We must have just passed a hot spring," Buck stated. "Probably the one where we filmed those fumaroles. We stopped there just before we filmed the Artists' Paintpots."

"I can smell them," Toni said, then she studied the map again. "It will be another twenty minutes or so until we get to where we will either go toward Grand Prismatic and Old Faithful or turn toward the west entrance."

"Toni! I think I know where we're going!" Buck suddenly exclaimed. "Lyall wants to poison the Wapiti pack! Remember, Isabel told us about them our first day here."

"That's right!" Toni said. "She said their den is near a spring just north of Grand Prismatic!"

"Yeah," Buck said. "It was a Spanish-sounding name."

"Here it is—Ojo Caliente Spring—at the end of a side road called Fountain Flat Drive that goes along the Firehole River," Toni said as she pointed to the spot. "So if he is going after the Wapiti pack, he'll go toward Grand Prismatic, and then in another fifteen minutes, he'll take a right onto the drive."

"See that? There's a bike trail there," Buck said. He pointed to a dotted line that had an icon of a bicycle on it. "It goes from the end of Fountain Flat Drive to Grand Prismatic. How long do you think it is?"

"From the map's scale, I'm guessing about three miles," Toni said. "Why?"

"I think I've got a plan," Buck said. "When we get there, we'll keep quiet until he starts preparing a bundle of kibble. Then we'll make a noise. When he comes to investigate, we'll jump out and break his drone."

"Why wait for him to get the kibble ready?" Toni said. "He might load it into the payload claw and drop it for the wolves before he comes back here to investigate."

"If he finds out we're here before getting the kibble ready, we won't have any proof that he's poisoning wolves," Buck explained. "He could just say he stopped to see the spring. We have to catch him in the act."

"But we know he has the right kind of drone and the

kibble," Toni said.

"He could easily get rid of the kibble," Buck said. "Then all he has is a drone in his truck. There's nothing wrong with that as long as he's not flying it. It's like Isabel said—he has to be caught red-handed."

"He could still get rid of the kibble after finding us," Toni said. "It would just be our word against his—no proof."

"Yeah, you're right," Buck said disappointedly. He was quiet for a moment but then smiled. He reached into the pocket of his cargo pants and pulled out his camera. "We'd have proof if we get pictures."

"That might work," Toni said skeptically. "So, *if* we're able to get out and *if* we get some pictures and *if* we're able to somehow break his drone—that's a lot of ifs—but if we can do all that, then what?"

"We run," Buck said.

"So now we have another if," Toni said. "What if he catches us?"

"He can't catch both of us if we run two different directions," Buck said. "I can run down the bike trail. There will be lots of people at Grand Prismatic that could help. And you can run up the drive to the main road. There will be a bunch of people driving toward Old Faithful to flag down for help."

"Hmm," Toni said. She stared at the map for a few seconds without saying anything more, then looked up at Buck. "I guess it *could* work, but it doesn't mean it *will*."

"Do you have a better idea?" Buck asked.

"No," Toni admitted.

Buck glanced out the window as they went around a curve.

"We're heading toward Grand Prismatic," Buck said. "We just passed a sign saying West Entrance, turn left."

Toni let out a sigh. "I was hoping he'd just leave the park and not go after any more wolves."

"Here," Buck said, pulling his camera from his pocket. "I'll go after the drone. You try to take a picture."

"Okay," Toni said. "If Fountain Flat Drive is where we're going, we've only got about fifteen more minutes, so we better get ready while we can."

"What do you mean?" Buck asked. "What's there to

get ready?"

"We don't know exactly where he'll stop. It could be at that picnic area near the start of the drive," Toni said, pointing to an icon with a picnic table. Then she pointed to another icon, one with a large *P*, at the end of the drive. "Or it could be at the parking area at the end."

"So?" Buck asked. "What difference does it make where he parks?"

"The drive is only about a mile long. We might have just a few seconds after he turns off onto the drive," Toni said. "But at most, only a couple of minutes. I'm clearing an exit route now so we can get out of here without climbing over that trunk."

"Good thinking," Buck said.

Toni rolled over on her back, her head on the truck bed. Scooting toward the trunk, she grabbed hold of the handle at the end and pulled the trunk until it was up against the front of the truck bed. When she finished, Buck moved back behind the generator, putting his head on the wheel well. Toni quickly folded the map, stuffed it into her backpack, and looped her arm through one of the shoulder straps. As she slid over beside Buck, the truck slowed down and turned. Buck and Toni looked at each other.

"Is your heart beating as hard as mine is?" Toni asked, holding tight to Buck's camera.

"Probably harder," Buck admitted.

"I don't think it could," Toni said.

"Just keep thinking about why we're doing this," Buck said. "We couldn't save Odin, but we can save the Wapiti pack."

TAKE 24:

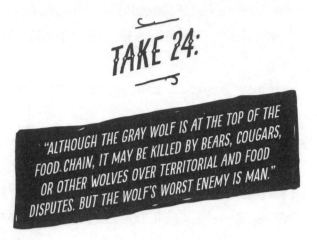

"ALTHOUGH THE GRAY WOLF IS AT THE TOP OF THE FOOD CHAIN, IT MAY BE KILLED BY BEARS, COUGARS, OR OTHER WOLVES OVER TERRITORIAL AND FOOD DISPUTES. BUT THE WOLF'S WORST ENEMY IS MAN."

The truck turned right onto Fountain Flat Drive but now continued at a slow pace.

"I counted to sixty in my head," Buck said, "and we haven't stopped yet. I'm sure we're past the picnic area by now. So we must be heading to the parking area."

The two silently watched through the shell's passenger-side window, seeing nothing but sky and occasional puffs of steam.

"Are you sure the drive's only a mile long?" Buck asked. "It seems like it's taking forever." He had barely gotten the words out when the truck slowed even more, turned left, and stopped. Then it moved in reverse and stopped again. The engine shut off. Suddenly sunlight filled the cab. The driver's-side door slammed, and the cab dimmed.

Buck and Toni quietly sat up and looked out the windows. Lyall had gone to the front of the truck but just stood there, looking around. The parking area of Fountain Flat Drive had a row of pull-in parking spaces lined up on one side of the road. The truck was backed into the last space. Across from it the pavement made a turnaround loop, but the road continued on past the loop for another hundred feet, where the pavement changed to gravel. At that point, several wooden posts blocked vehicles from driving onto what had once been the continuation of the road. Beyond the posts was a trailhead sign, and in the distance down the trail billowing plumes of steam rose in the air.

"That must be the start of the bike trail," Buck said. "It just looks like an old gravel road."

"I guess at one time you could drive all the way to Grand Prismatic from here," Toni said. "And I'm guessing the steam is from Ojo Caliente."

Buck looked around the generator and out the back window. The Firehole River was about half a football field from the truck. Between them and the river was a flat field with sparse tufts of short, dried-up-looking grasses and weeds. Dozens of fallen pieces of timber lay criss-crossed in the weeds, their barkless trunks long and eerie white. Puffs of steam dotted the riverbank as well as the broad valley beyond. Hills and then mountains rose up on the other side of the valley.

"I guess the Wapiti pack is out there somewhere," Toni said, looking over Buck's shoulder. Then she looked back toward the front of the truck. "Lyall's going over toward those posts."

"Maybe he wants to make sure nobody is coming down the trail," Buck said.

"Do you think our plan will work?" Toni asked.

"I hope so," Buck answered. "I'll go out first, but I won't be able to get out easily if I'm sitting down. I think if I tuck down on my hands and knees like in tornado drill position, I'll be able to either charge out of here or duck down."

"Good idea, but be quiet and try not to let the truck wiggle," Toni said.

Getting on his hands and knees, Buck carefully backed up behind the generator until his feet touched the side of the truck. Then he ducked down as low as he could, his weight resting on his forearms that lay against the truck bed, his forehead resting on his wrists.

"Am I low enough?" he asked. "I don't want him to be able to see me from the cab."

"You're good," Toni said, and got into the same position. Then, raising their heads, the two watched through the side window as Lyall approached the truck.

"He's whistling again," Buck said.

"Yeah, the same tune," Toni stated.

Lyall walked to the cab's passenger door, and the kids ducked down. When the passenger door slammed, they glanced up for just a second, seeing Lyall walk past the shell's window and on around to the back of the truck. The strap of the GERUMAC pack was looped over one shoulder. The whistling stopped when Lyall reached the back of the truck, and the kids ducked once again. There was a quiet click at the back, and the shell's door squeaked as it opened. A second later the tailgate dropped down, and a stream of sunlight poured across the strip of truck bed next to the generator and across the trunk.

"Huh," Lyall muttered to himself, "the trunk must have slid forward."

Buck and Toni held their breaths, but the man didn't inspect the inside of the truck bed. Instead there were some softer sounds, as if things had been placed on the tailgate.

The generator sat on short stubby legs, leaving about a three-inch gap between the bottom of the plastic-encased motor and the truck bed. By placing his cheek on the truck bed, Buck looked through the gap. The bottom part of a gray hoodie was all he could see of Lyall, but sitting on the tailgate in front of the man was the bag of kibble and a box of tissues.

Buck watched as Lyall's hand reached behind him and came out with a pair of yellow rubber gloves. After putting them on, the man took a tissue from the box and laid it on the tailgate. Then, unrolling the top of the kibble bag, he reached in and pulled out a handful of dog food. He placed the kibble onto the center of the tissue, added a few more pieces, then gathered the corners of the tissue and gave it a twist.

Lyall set the bundle aside and slid the drone's pack across the tailgate until it was in front of him. Now the pack blocked Buck's line of vision, but Buck could hear it being unzipped. He slowly rotated his head until his mouth was right up against Toni's ear.

"He's made a bundle of kibble," he whispered, "and he's getting out the drone."

As Buck whispered, there was a series of three electronic beeps and then the sound of footsteps moving away from the truck. Buck slowly peeked around the end of the generator. Lyall had squatted down about ten feet from the truck. He smoothed out an area of ground with his hand and set the drone on it. Then he smoothed out another spot about three feet from the drone and placed the bundle in the middle of it. As the man stood up, Buck ducked back behind the generator.

"You ready?" he whispered.

Toni nodded.

When Toni nodded, Buck sprang from his position. Lyall had turned and was coming back toward the truck. Buck couldn't stand totally upright without hitting his head, but he went as fast as he could while leaning over. As he rushed around the generator, Lyall had a startled look on his face. But by the time Buck was on the tailgate, the look had changed to one of comprehension, and the man charged toward him. As Buck tried to jump from the tailgate, Lyall reached out, his hand grabbing at Buck's leg. Buck went sprawling, landing face-first on the ground.

When Buck sprang from his hiding position, Toni had turned the camera on and followed after him. But she never had a chance to snap a picture. When Buck went flying off the tailgate in front of her, Lyall moved quickly. He gave her a shove, and as she stumbled backward, Lyall pushed the tailgate shut. The open bag of kibble spilled into the truck bed, pieces rolling under the generator.

By the time Toni was back to the tailgate again, Lyall had pulled Buck up, twisting the boy's arm tightly behind his back. Buck's face was scratched and his nose bleeding. Lyall yanked Buck toward the tailgate and stood with his body blocking any chance of Toni scrambling out.

"Let me go!" Buck yelled, trying to squirm out of the man's grasp.

"Calm down, Buck," Lyall said, putting more upward pressure on Buck's arm.

"Ow!" Buck exclaimed, but instantly stopped struggling. He wiped the blood dripping down his chin with the sleeve of his free arm.

"What are you two doing here?" Lyall asked.

"Why did you poison Odin?" Toni demanded, ignoring Lyall's question.

"So you figured it all out, didn't you? Well, it's a real simple reason. I don't like predators," Lyall stated as easily as if he had said he didn't like grape-bubble-gum ice cream. "They kill livestock. Last year, five sheep were killed by wolves on my ranch. And other ranchers have had problems with them too. I'm simply protecting my investments and helping out my neighbors."

"The wolves in the park didn't kill your sheep," Buck

said defensively, still locked in Lyall's grip.

"You don't know that," Lyall said. "Wolves roam."

"Isabel said there are hunting seasons in all three states around the park. Why not just hunt them legally?" Toni tried to reason.

So far there had been no anger in Lyall's voice—no irritation or even a hint of concern. He didn't sound any different from how he had during the drone-flying class or the conversation around the campfire. Now Lyall just laughed.

"A few wolves each year? That would hardly take care of the problem. And if people like Isabel hadn't brought the wolves back to begin with, there wouldn't even be a problem," Lyall stated. "But now I've got another problem. You two. When I saw you this morning on the hill, I was worried you would cause trouble, but I never thought you'd stow away in my truck. You gave me quite a surprise."

"Did you kill wolves from the Gardner pack, too?" Buck asked, his voice filled with rage.

Lyall shrugged. "I don't know. They weren't around the

den, and I didn't want to waste battery time waiting for them to come back. I wasn't able to charge my batteries up again last night because I came to your cookout. But I needed to see how much anyone knew. And Lobo saved me some time letting me know they closed Slough Creek Road."

"So you *were* planning on going to go back to kill the other Slough Creek wolves!" Toni cried out.

"Of course," Lyall said. "I wanted to finish what you guys screwed up for me."

"What kind of plans did we mess up?" Buck said. "We didn't even know you were at the Slough Creek Campground."

"Ah, so you've figured out where I was hiding, too," Lyall said pleasantly. "You two are pretty smart. So, have you figured out how I found Odin?"

Buck had a fair idea of how that happened, but it seemed Lyall wanted a chance to brag about his malicious actions. *If I can keep him talking,* Buck thought, *maybe someone will drive down here and we'll have some help.*

"No, I guess we're not that smart," Buck said. "So how

did you find him?"

"That was pure luck," Lyall said, falling for the bait. "My original plan was to drop the kibble by the den as soon as the spotters left that day."

"You were even going to kill the pups?" Toni said with alarm.

"A wolf is a wolf," Lyall said. "Those pups will grow up to be adult killers. Anyway, I had my drone flying that direction when I saw the wolves trotting across the hillside. Two went down the hill, but the big gray one was interested in the drone, so I dropped the kibble for it. He was a little leery at first but finally went to investigate it. I watched him gobble it up, then went to find the other two. They were just about to take down that injured elk."

Toni gasped. "You mean Odin was dying up there while we were watching the elk kill?"

"Yeah, I saw you guys down there at the ranger station," Lyall said. "I thought as soon as you left, I would follow through with my original plan and drop a treat near the den for the rest of the pack. But you guys came snooping around the Slough Creek campground and put an end to that. Now the rangers are watching the Slough Creek pack like hawks."

"I'm glad," Toni said defiantly. "Wolves have just as much right to live as you do. They don't deserve to be killed."

"Wolves do more killing than I do," Lyall said. "I'm just helping protect their prey. Just think of the poor sheep and cattle, not to mention all the elk and bison I'm saving."

"It's all part of nature," Buck argued, "part of the natural food chain."

"Well, I'm just removing a few links," Lyall said.

"You're evil!" Toni exclaimed.

"No," Lyall said. "It's the wolf that's always evil. I'm sure you've heard of *The Three Little Pigs* or *Little Red Riding Hood*?"

"Those are only stories," Buck said.

"I'm just playing the same role as the hunter who came to rescue the sick old grandmother from the big, bad wolf. And now I'm going to save some wapiti from the Wapiti pack." Lyall chuckled.

"I don't see anything funny about it," Buck said.

"Oh, but it's a lot of fun taking pictures of wildlife up close," Lyall said. "You get all kinds of interesting action shots when the animals spot the drones."

"You almost killed Buck getting your action shot of the bison," Toni said angrily.

"We saw your drone on Shoop's video."

"I didn't intend to get them charging, but I got some really awesome video out of it," Lyall said. "Maybe your dads would be willing to pay for my videos—they could use them for your show. My video of Odin is pretty good, too."

"They'd never do that!" Toni said.

"Too bad—it'd be a nice addition," Lyall said. "But enough time has been wasted talking. I need to drop a treat for the Wapiti before someone comes along."

TAKE 25:

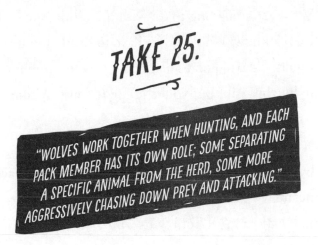

"WOLVES WORK TOGETHER WHEN HUNTING, AND EACH PACK MEMBER HAS ITS OWN ROLE; SOME SEPARATING A SPECIFIC ANIMAL FROM THE HERD, SOME MORE AGGRESSIVELY CHASING DOWN PREY AND ATTACKING."

Up until now, Buck had stood there with his arm twisted around his back, not only because it hurt if he moved, but he also wanted to know why Lyall was killing the wolves. Now he glanced up the road, hoping Lyall's concerns would come true—that someone would come along. But the road was deserted and so was the bike trail.

"We're not going to let you do this!" Buck exclaimed, trying even though it hurt to break away from Lyall's grip.

"Calm down!" Lyall said, his grip on Buck tightening once again. Buck stopped struggling.

"What are you going to do with us?" Toni asked.

"I don't know. I'm going to have to think about that," Lyall said. "You're good kids, and I have no intention of really hurting you, but you're going to have to cooperate with me."

"No way!" Buck declared.

"Buck, he's right," Toni said. "We *are* going to have to cooperate with him."

Buck looked up at Toni with a puzzled expression, but Lyall laughed.

"Girls are always more sensible than boys," the man said. "You need to listen to her, Buck."

"It's the *only* way it will work," Toni said, looking directly at Buck.

Buck's eyes met Toni's, and she gave an almost imperceptible nod.

"Okay," Buck said. "I'll cooperate."

Lyall still had Buck's arm twisted up behind his back, but now he moved the boy around until Buck was standing right up against the tailgate, facing it.

"Toni, scoot back in there away from the tailgate,"

Lyall said. Toni did as he instructed.

"Okay, Buck," the man continued. "I'm going to let go of you, but you have to climb into the truck."

When Buck started to step onto the truck's bumper, Lyall let go of his arm. Once Buck's body blocked Lyall's view of Toni, Toni quickly gave Buck a quick shake of her head and mouthed, *Don't get in.* Then she held up her hand to her cheek, extending her thumb out toward her ear and her pinkie toward her mouth, while closing the other three fingers. She immediately made another gesture, sweeping her hand across in front of her and quickly closing her fist like she was grabbing at something. Buck gave Toni a quick nod to indicate he understood.

Instead of swinging his leg into the truck, Buck quickly stepped back down and, pushing back against Lyall, reached over to the tailgate latch and pulled up. The tailgate fell open. As Lyall grabbed at Buck's arm, Buck jerked away from him, spun around, and pushed himself up to sit on the tailgate, his legs dangling over the edge.

"I thought you were going to cooperate." For the first time, Lyall sounded irritated.

"I am—but I'm not going back in there," Buck stated emphatically. "I'll sit right here."

"All right, have it your way, but you've got to turn around and face the truck and sit on your hands," Lyall said, his tone now threatening. "And neither one of you better try anything."

As Buck turned around, crisscrossing his legs, Lyall reached up to the shell door and pulled it down. Then Lyall took his phone from his back pocket and sat on the tailgate, again blocking Toni's way out. As he turned on his phone, Toni crawled back into the space beside the generator. She knew neither Buck nor Lyall could see her through the shell door's window, but they could hear her. She made sure the camera's flash was turned off and then aimed it, catching the side of Lyall's head and the drone and bundle of kibble in the distance.

"It just occurred to me what you were whistling," Toni said loudly. "It's from *Peter and the Wolf*, isn't it?" As she spoke she snapped the picture, hoping her voice covered the sound of the camera clicking.

Lyall chuckled. "So you know that story, huh? Fitting,

isn't it?"

"Yeah, but the hunters don't kill the wolf," Toni said, zooming in and snapping a close-up of the drone and kibble. "They take him to a zoo."

"Well, this story ends differently," Lyall stated. He pushed something on his phone screen, waited a few seconds, and then turned the phone around so Buck could see it. "Since you're here, you might as well have another flying lesson. Tapping this icon makes the cargo claw open and close."

Still sitting on his hands, Buck leaned over and looked at the phone's screen. As he had seen in class, there were the two circles that were used to fly the drone. There were also several small icons lined up across the top of the screen. Lyall pointed to one that looked like the claw.

"Would my ace student like to see too?" Lyall asked as he held the phone up above his shoulder, the screen facing the window. Then Lyall put the phone back in front of him and flamboyantly tapped the icon with his index finger. Buck turned and looked over his shoulder, watching the red claw on the bottom of the GERUMAC open. Lyall moved his thumbs around on the screen, and the drone's rotors started spinning. The drone lifted about ten feet into the air, made a small circle around the area, and then hovered directly above the bundle of kibble.

"Wicked-looking, isn't it?" Lyall said. Neither Buck nor Toni said a word as the drone descended until the landing skids touched the ground on either side of the bundle. Lyall tapped at the icon again, and the claw closed around its cargo.

"How do you get the video to work?" Buck asked.

"I knew you'd be interested," Lyall said, smiling. "This camera icon right here. Tap it and it will take a single photo. Hold it for a second, and the video camera will come on until you tap it again."

Lyall turned the phone toward Buck. Keeping his hands under his butt, Buck took a couple of scoots closer to the man.

"What are you doing?" Lyall said, and instantly pulled the phone back.

"Just getting closer," Buck stated. "I couldn't see."

"Okay." Lyall turned the phone toward Buck again.

Buck leaned over even closer to the phone, and although he kept his head angled down like he was looking at the phone, he quickly glanced up at the window with his eyes and then back down. At the same time, he gave a small nod, hoping Toni would catch his signal to be ready. But before Buck could make his move, Lyall pulled the phone back.

"Watch," the man said. Lyall flew the drone over to the trailhead sign and made it hover in front of it. He tapped the icon, then landed the drone at the base of the sign. When the rotors stopped spinning, he held the phone out for Buck to see once more. Lyall had taken a picture of a sign tacked on the post under the trail information. On the phone's screen, Buck saw an icon of a drone with a red circle around it and a red line angled across. Under the icon were the words REMOTE-CONTROLLED AIRCRAFT PROHIBITED.

"Ironic, isn't it?" Lyall chuckled.

"Let me see," Toni said, but when Lyall held the phone up, this time he did so over his left shoulder, out of Buck's reach.

"So, now to find the wolves," Lyall said, but instead of

starting up the drone again, he pulled out a piece of paper from his shirt pocket. "I ran into some wolf spotters the other day, and they were so nice. They gave me the exact coordinates of where the Wapiti den is. All I have to do is set the GPS coordinates and it will go right to it. I'll drop its cargo—"

"You mean poison!" Toni interrupted.

"Its cargo," Lyall repeated, ignoring Toni's comment. "And then all I have to do is push the GPS icon again, and it will automatically return to its starting coordinates."

"No, please don't. You don't need to kill any others," Toni cried, but Lyall ignored her again.

"Forty-four degrees, thirty-four feet, and twenty-three inches north," he stated, reading off and then punching in the coordinates on his phone. "One hundred ten degrees, fifty-four feet, and five inches west. That ought to take us right to the den."

Lyall tapped on the screen but this time didn't touch the circles on his phone. Buck looked over his right shoulder and saw the drone automatically lift up thirty feet in the air and then quickly fly away. Buck turned to look over his left shoulder and watched it as it headed toward the Firehole River. Then he leaned over toward Lyall and looked down at the phone in the man's hands.

"I knew you couldn't resist watching," Lyall said. He turned the phone slightly so both he and Buck could see the screen. "All we have to do now is sit back and watch. It will be a few minutes."

On the screen, Buck saw the video the drone was taking as it flew over the river. On the other side, it went over a marshy area and then past an area dotted with puffs of steam rising from bright blue springs that were surrounded by the white crusty deposits. Buck looked over his left shoulder again in the direction the drone had taken. He could no longer see it.

Buck and Toni said nothing, but Lyall kept on talking. "Once it gets nearly there, I'll have to take it off GPS and fly it myself; otherwise, it will just land right on top of the den site. I'll figure out exactly where I want to drop the cargo and . . ."

It's now or never, Buck thought as Lyall continued talking. Still half-turned and looking over his left shoulder, he quietly pulled his left hand out from under him. Then rapidly swinging his arm around toward the front of his body, he rotated, simultaneously rising up on left foot and right knee. Without pausing, Buck reached out for the phone with his left hand while extending his right arm and catching the edge of the tailgate to support himself and keep from falling off.

Buck moved so quickly, he had already pivoted completely around and was reaching for the phone before Lyall could even move. But as Buck grabbed at the phone, Lyall reached out for the boy. At the same time, there was the squeak of the shell's door as Toni forcefully pushed it open. With Buck kneeling down and leaning over as he reached toward the phone, the door easily swung up over the boy's shoulder, hitting Lyall in the back of the head. The unexpected blow gave Buck the chance to snatch the phone and roll off over the edge of the tailgate. Then Buck quickly scrambled to his feet and ran.

Lyall yelled out at him, cussing at the top of his lungs, but Buck charged toward the bike trail. He heard the tailgate slam shut behind him but kept running, passing the posts that barricaded the trail from vehicles. Approaching the trailhead sign, he saw several places listed but only had a chance to focus on the top one: OJO CALIENTE SPRING—.2 MILE. As he passed the sign, he heard footsteps running after him. Buck knew it wasn't Toni. She would have called out. Buck pumped his legs harder, his heart pounding in his chest.

He soon passed a small side trail that led off to the right with a sign saying OJO CALIENTE SPRING. The area was covered with thick steam, and a slight breeze pushed it across the bike trail. Buck ran through it.

Once past the steam, Buck glanced at the phone. He pushed the GPS icon several times, hoping it would turn off and the GERUMAC would not know where to fly. Then he slid his thumb rapidly back and forth across one of the circles.

I hope that crushed it! he thought.

With one last click, he turned off the phone. The screen went black. Buck slipped the phone into the pocket of his hoodie and kept running. Ahead was a footbridge crossing the Firehole River. He picked up his pace, and soon his feet were stomping rapidly and rhythmically across the wooden boards. Reaching the other side, Buck started counting his paces. He counted forty-seven before he heard the first thud of a running footstep on the bridge behind him.

He's probably about fifty yards behind me, Buck thought. *About half a football field.*

Even though his lungs were burning and his legs aching, Buck pumped harder. Ahead was another side trail. QUEEN'S LAUNDRY—1.4 was written on its trail sign, and an arrow pointed right. It also said GRAND PRISMATIC SPRING—2.7, and an arrow pointed up. Buck kept running straight ahead.

On either side of the trail the ground was covered with crusty white mineral deposits surrounding bright blue pools of boiling water. Steam rose from the hot springs, and orange and yellow rivulets flowed from them. Just as there had been behind the truck, fallen timber lay everywhere—long, barkless trees, smooth and bleached white from the acids and heat of surrounding springs. Here and there, some still stood, like skeletal sentries, warning not to step off the path.

Buck kept going but knew his pace was slowing down. He could hear footsteps closing in behind him.

"You won't be able to outrun me, Buck!" Lyall yelled. The voice seemed less than half the distance behind Buck than before.

Buck once again tried to increase his pace, but a pain in his side felt like it would split him apart, like the cracks and fissures that belched sulfuric steam in the hostile environment around him. Ahead, the trail curved sharply to the left. As Buck took the curve, he suddenly heard a loud, sharp crack behind him. Immediately there was a splash and then an ear-piercing scream.

Buck stopped and turned to look, instantly grasping the horrifying situation. In trying to take advantage of the curve, Lyall had gone off the trail to angle directly toward Buck and catch him. Buck could see Lyall. The man had gone about five yards when suddenly the ground broke through and his left leg submerged into the boiling water below. His right knee had not broken through and was still on top of the layer of mineral deposits. The man's hands were clawing at the ground, desperately trying to pull himself out, but the crusty deposits were crumbling in his fingers. All the while Lyall was screaming, a horrible painful shriek.

Buck quickly looked around. A long-dead tree, white and barkless, lay alongside the trail. Buck rushed to it and tried to pick up one end. It was almost too heavy to lift, but he managed to get his arms around it. He dragged it about fifteen feet until it was on the trail beside the screaming man. Then, being careful not to step off the trail, Buck maneuvered the heavy timber until it lay perpendicular to the trail, part of it resting on the crusty surface. He kept working, slowly getting the tree to move, inch by inch, toward Lyall. Finally there was enough room on the trail that Buck could get on his hands and knees and push at the end of the heavy timber. He shoved, and shoved, and shoved again, until the other end was within Lyall's reach.

"Grab it," Buck yelled out over the man's screams. "Use it to pull yourself out!"

Lyall grabbed hold of the log and slowly started pulling

himself out, one hand reaching ahead of the other, pulling his way back to solid ground, while his injured leg dragged uselessly behind him. Finally the man got close enough that Buck could safely grab one of his arms. As Buck pulled, the man's remaining strength seemed to drain from him, and he collapsed on the trail. Buck didn't waste any time. He pulled Lyall's phone from his pocket, turned it back on, and then punched in 9-1-1.

"I need a medical helicopter!" Buck cried out as soon as a woman answered. "A man has fallen into a hot spring on the Fountain Flat Trail, not too far from where the Queen's Laundry Trail turns off."

Buck paused for a second while the woman spoke, then he continued. "I think he's unconscious. His left leg is severely burned, and his hands, too. But there's more. You also need to get ahold of Lobo—Chuck Donaldson—he's the park's biologist in charge of the wolf restoration project. Tell him to bring a helicopter here as quick as he can too. Someone was trying to poison some more wolves."

TAKE 26:

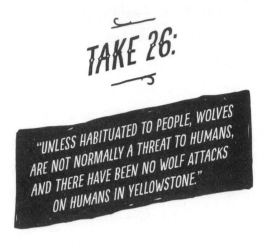

"UNLESS HABITUATED TO PEOPLE, WOLVES ARE NOT NORMALLY A THREAT TO HUMANS, AND THERE HAVE BEEN NO WOLF ATTACKS ON HUMANS IN YELLOWSTONE."

Buck took off his sweatshirt and draped it over Lyall, trying to keep him as warm as possible. Then he sat down on the end of the log and waited. He wondered if Toni had gotten out of the truck, and if so, how far she had gotten. He also wondered about how far the GERUMAC had gone, whether it had crashed, and especially, whether or not any wolves had discovered the poisoned kibble. He looked at Lyall, who lay there breathing with difficulty. The man's hands were blistered with burns. Buck refused to even glance toward his leg.

"I don't understand," he said to the unconscious man, "how you could be so nice with everyone at the drone competition yesterday and yet be so cruel, viciously killing wolves."

Maybe there's still a chance to keep any other animals from dying, Buck suddenly thought. *Lyall said the drone would automatically return to the original coordinates.*

Buck turned on the phone and brought up the drone's app. He clicked on the GPS button. There were no coordinates listed.

"Darn!" Buck said. "They must have erased when I turned it off."

Buck zipped the phone into one of his cargo pants pockets. Then, crossing his arms on his knees, he leaned over, rested his head on his arms, and waited.

It wasn't more than ten minutes before he heard the sound of a helicopter coming his direction from over the mountains to the west. Buck stood up and, as it approached, waved his arms over his head. The helicopter, with a big red cross on its side, landed nearby on a wide section in the trail. The skids had barely touched down when a man wearing medical scrubs jumped out. He grabbed a large first aid kit from the chopper and rushed to Lyall's side. A woman, also wearing scrubs, jumped out too. She reached back in and pulled out a long orange plastic board with straps fastened across it.

"You've been bleeding. Are you hurt, too?" the man asked Buck as he opened the kit and took out a stethoscope.

"No, I'm fine," Buck said. "Just a nosebleed."

"Okay," the man said, handing Buck his hoodie. "What's his name?"

"Lyall Griffith," Buck answered.

The woman brought the board over and laid it alongside Lyall. Then the two medics turned Lyall over.

"Is he your father?" the woman asked as she started unfastening all the straps on the board.

"No, he's not related to me," Buck stated, but he didn't elaborate.

The man pulled the stethoscope from his ears and, letting it hang around his neck, quickly took a vial and syringe from the first aid kit.

"I'm giving him morphine to relieve the pain," the man said to the woman. She took a small notebook from the kit and recorded what was being done. As soon as the medic had given Lyall the shot, he turned again to Buck. "We're going to lift him. Could you push the board under him?"

"Sure," Buck said.

The woman went to Lyall's feet, the man to his shoulders. "On the count of three," the woman said. "One, two, three."

The medics lifted Lyall, and Buck pushed the board under him. Then the medics laid Lyall on top of it.

"When you called nine one one, they radioed in for a ranger to come too. One should be at the parking lot soon," the woman said to Buck as she covered Lyall with a blanket and quickly fastened the straps around him. "Will you be able to get back there okay by yourself, or should we wait?"

"I'll be able to get back. There's no need for you to wait," Buck said. As he spoke he could hear the wail of a siren echoing up the river valley.

The man positioned himself at Lyall's head, the woman at his feet, and on the count of three, they lifted the board and hurried toward the waiting helicopter. They slid the board into the back of the helicopter and then climbed in. Within seconds the helicopter lifted and flew away. The entire evacuation had lasted less than five minutes.

For a few seconds Buck watched the chopper fly, then he turned and ran—past the Queen's Laundry Trail, over the bridge, and through the steam of Ojo Caliente Spring. Finally he could see Lyall's pickup. The tailgate was closed, but the shell door was open. Beyond it, a ranger's SUV was racing toward him, its lights flashing, sirens shrieking. Although exhausted, Buck picked up his speed.

The SUV drove past the pickup, stopping beside the posts. Isabel and Toni jumped out and ran past the posts, meeting Buck a few feet down the trail.

"Are you okay?" Isabel said as she and Toni both grabbed Buck in a hug.

"I'm okay," Buck answered, hugging them back. Then he stepped away and turned to Toni. "What about you?

Are you all right?"

"I'm fine," Toni said. "When you ran, Lyall pushed me back inside and slammed the tailgate and door before he took off after you."

"How did you get out?" Buck said. "He didn't lock it?"

"No," Toni said. "He must have forgotten he hadn't locked it, because after he shoved me back, he said at least I wasn't going anywhere."

"So what happened with Lyall?" Isabel asked, but before Buck had time to answer, another helicopter came flying up, this one from the north, following Fountain Flat Drive. As the chopper started to land in the center of the turnaround loop, Buck ran toward it. He was at the chopper's door before the rotors had even quit spinning. Toni and Isabel were right on his heels.

"Lyall poisoned Odin," Buck blurted out as soon as Lobo opened the door. "He used a drone, and I think he dropped some for the Gardner pack, too. Now his drone is out there someplace with another load of poisoned kibble intended for the Wapiti pack. He had GPS set to automatically take it to the den, but I tried to crash the drone before it got there."

Lobo jumped out of the chopper. "I've heard most of that—Toni told me over Isabel's radio," he said. "Are you okay?"

"Yes," Buck said. "I'm fine. But we need to find that drone."

"It probably has a recall button," the pilot called through the open door. "We might be able to get it to fly right back to us."

"I tried," Buck said, disappointment in his voice, "but the coordinates were deleted when I turned off the phone."

"Don't worry," Toni said. "I wrote them down in the dust on Lyall's window!"

"Super!" the pilot called out to her. "We'll be able to follow the exact path the drone was set for. It might help us locate the drone faster."

"And if there is a wolf down," Lobo added, "we may be able to save him, or at least not let him suffer."

"I'll go write them down," Toni said, and ran toward Lyall's truck.

Buck looked at Lobo. "Can Toni and I go with you?"

"Of course—we'll need all the eyes we can get," Lobo said, then turned to Isabel. "I'm afraid there won't be room for you, though."

"That's okay," Isabel said. "Can you take the kids back to Mammoth when you're done? I'll call their dads, and we'll all meet at your office. We can go over everything there."

"That will be fine," Lobo said. "Will you call in and have someone check the Gardner pack?"

"Right away," Isabel said.

When Toni returned, she gave the pilot a page from her sketchbook, where she had written down the coordinates. Then she turned to Isabel.

"The kibble is in the back of Lyall's pickup," she told the ranger. "But some spilled out onto the ground when the tailgate was opened. It's already laced with poison, so don't touch it."

"Thanks, I'll take care of it," Isabel said. "And I'll make sure none is left lying around that other animals may get into."

"What happened to Lyall?" Toni then asked Buck as the pilot punched the coordinates into the helicopter's GPS.

"He went off the trail trying to cut me off on a curve," Buck said, "but he broke through and ended up falling into one of the hot springs."

"Ooh, that's horrible," Isabel said, shuddering at the thought.

"Medics took him away in a helicopter ambulance," Buck continued. "He's seriously injured. How far did you get, Toni?"

"Almost to the picnic area," she answered.

"That's where I found her," Isabel added, "running up the road."

The pilot turned on the helicopter's engine. Buck, Toni, and Lobo ducked under the spinning rotors then climbed in. As the helicopter lifted, Buck looked out the window at the brilliant blue spring.

"That must be Ojo Caliente," he stated. "I ran right past it."

"Yes, it's Spanish for 'Hot Eye,'" Lobo said, "because of its shape."

The helicopter flew over the same route the drone had taken—over the river, the marsh, and the scrubby sage area that Buck and Toni had seen on the video. But now, without the limit of the drone's camera's angle, they could see all around them. The land was dotted with hot springs and mud pots, but gradually became more stable as the chopper moved toward the hills and mountains beyond.

Toni reached into her backpack, pulled out Buck's binoculars, and handed them to him. Lobo reached into the console between him and the pilot and brought out two more pairs. He handed a set to Toni.

"I'll scan the front. Buck, you take the left, and, Toni, you keep watch to the right," he said. They all kept their eyes toward the ground as the helicopter flew on.

"We're getting close to where the coordinates end," the pilot announced after several minutes. "Did you see anything?"

"No," the three stated together.

"I'll fly over it again," the pilot said, and the chopper started to turn.

"Wait a second! I see something!" Toni exclaimed. The

pilot immediately hovered the aircraft. "On the side of that hill. See that barren area surrounded by low bushes? There's a wolf!"

"I see it! It's alive!" Buck shouted.

"I do too! And it looks healthy. Good eyes, Toni!" Lobo said, then he turned to the pilot. "Don't go any closer. We don't want to disturb it."

The wolf stood erect, looking up as the helicopter hovered in place for a few seconds. Then the animal turned and disappeared into a dark spot in the middle of the barren area.

"It just went into its den," Toni said.

"We've got to find that drone," Lobo said. "Turn around and sweep the chopper back and forth along the coordinate path."

They went back all the way to the river without seeing anything else.

"It might be way off course," Buck told the pilot. "I turned off the GPS and tried to crash the drone before it could get to the den. Who knows where it ended up?"

The pilot turned and made longer sweeps, back and

forth, as they made their way toward the den again. They were on the last long sweep before once more reaching the den when Buck called out.

"I see something. A funny gray shape near that lone spruce tree."

The pilot headed toward where Buck directed.

"There!" Buck said. "You don't need binoculars to see it now."

The charcoal-gray drone sat at the edge of a mineral deposit surrounding a hot spring. The bundle of kibble was still in its red claw.

"You really did send that drone off course," the pilot stated, hovering the chopper above it.

"And you made a perfect landing, too!" Toni said.

"Well, I can't land here," the pilot said.

"It's not safe to walk to it either," Lobo said. He sighed and shook his head. "I sure wish we could get that drone, though. Besides needing it for evidence, I don't want that kibble left there. A wolf or other animal might still be able to get to it."

"Maybe Toni could fly the drone away from the spring,"

Buck suggested. "She was really good at it in class."

"In the park, Buck!" Toni said with alarm. "That's illegal!"

"I didn't think of that," Buck admitted, but Lobo laughed.

"I think we can make an exception in this case," he said, and turned to the pilot. "Land this thing as close as you safely can!"

The helicopter landed on the top of a treeless hill several hundred feet from the drone. They all got out and looked at the GERUMAC sitting spiderlike on the alien-looking landscape below, its dangerous cargo in its claw. Buck took Lyall's phone from his pocket. He brought up the app, and two circles appeared on the phone's screen. Buck held the phone out to Toni, but she didn't take it.

"Maybe you should fly it," she said to the pilot.

"I've never flown one," the pilot said.

Toni looked at Lobo. "Me neither," he said.

"Okay," Toni said, and she took the phone. "Here goes."

She barely touched the circles with her thumbs. The

drone's rotors started spinning, but the drone skittered sideways, its landing skids bouncing across the mineral deposits toward the spring. Toni instantly picked her thumbs up, and the drone stopped.

"Sorry," she said. "This thing is touchy."

Holding her breath, she tried again. This time the drone lifted straight up. It hovered for a second and then veered off away from them, going right across the boiling blue water.

"Oops, wrong way!" Toni said. She made the drone hover for a second and then moved it in a wide sweep around the spring, avoiding traveling over it again. Then the drone flew straight toward them, rising in elevation as it came to the hill. Toni landed it three feet in front of Buck, and they all cheered.

TAKE 27:

"A WOLF PACK IS A FAMILY. IT USUALLY HAS ONE BREEDING PAIR, THE OFFSPRING FROM PREVIOUS YEARS, AND THE CURRENT YEAR'S NEW LITTER OF PUPS."

It didn't take long to fly back to Mammoth, and soon the helicopter landed near the building across from the Albright Visitor Center. Isabel wasn't there yet, but the Green Beast was in the parking lot. Dad and Shoop came running up as soon as the rotors stopped. Philo was with them too.

"When Isabel called, we were shocked!" Dad said as Buck and Toni jumped out.

Both Dad and Shoop gave each of the kids a big hug.

"And when I heard your names mentioned on my

radio scanner," Philo added, "I rushed up to your campsite. Your dad was still on the phone with Isabel."

"Are you okay, Buck? You look terrible!" Shoop said.

"I'm fine. I just landed on my face," Buck said, reaching up and touching his sore nose. "Does it look bad? I haven't seen it."

"It's mostly dried blood," Toni said.

"I'll tell the camera you punched me," Buck teasingly told her.

"Well, I'd like to punch someone," Shoop said.

"Me too," Dad said. "I can't believe this! We trusted Lyall. We know he's the one who killed Odin, but why did he take off with you? Isabel didn't have many details."

"He didn't know we were in the back of his truck," Buck admitted. "We had seen his drone flying from where Lobo had said the Gardner pack's den was, and it looked like it was being flown from the trail near the amphitheater." Buck and Toni continued telling their story, ending with retrieving the drone by the hot spring.

"What about the Gardner pack?" Shoop said. "Were any of those wolves killed?"

"I don't know," Lobo answered. "A crew is checking them out, but I haven't heard back from them yet."

"Maybe there's something on Lyall's video that will help your crew locate the kibble," Toni suggested.

"Let's find out," Lobo said. "Come on into my office. It will be easier for us all to watch on my computer than on his phone."

As Lobo unlocked the building's door, Isabel drove in. They waited while she parked, and then they all went down the hall to Lobo's office. Lobo hooked the phone up to his computer.

"There are several different videos, but they are each dated," Lobo said. He clicked on the one dated May 18. On the screen, they saw what the drone had recorded earlier that morning. It flew from the trail above the amphitheater over Mammoth Campground, going directly over the Green Beast before it crossed the main road. Then it angled steeply upward toward the top of the tall cliff, the Gardner River flowing far below. Once over the cliff, it flew a few minutes to a ravine. It hovered over the ravine. Looking at the computer in Lobo's office, they all watched a white bundle drop and land by a small dugout.

"Is that the Gardner pack's den?" Toni said in alarm.

"Don't worry," Lobo said. "It was, but the pack moved its pups to a different den a couple of weeks ago."

"Lyall must not have known that," Isabel said.

"Thank goodness," Shoop said.

"I'll call this in to my crew," Lobo said. "They probably didn't search the old den area. They'll have that bundle picked up within minutes."

As Lobo spoke into his radio, the video continued, showing the drone's path as it flew back across the cliff and went down toward a hill. Then it turned, followed the cliff along the river, and turned again. Soon, it was hovering right above Buck and Toni, and for a second time, Buck watched himself staring up at a drone. Then the drone headed back across the road.

"Oh my!" Philo exclaimed as the video showed him standing by one of several RVs and campers lined up near the shed. "I never even noticed it fly over!"

The drone continued, flying over Philo's campsite,

then a gold truck with a camper in the bed on the upper tier, and then across an empty campsite. Past the camping area, it turned, staying just above the trees. It soon went over the amphitheater, followed the path, and descended onto the bench above the campground. A little redheaded boy standing near the gold pickup was the only camper who had even looked up at the drone.

Lobo had finished his call, and now he clicked on another video, this one dated May 16. Now they watched as the drone flew over an empty campground, across a creek, and up a hill beyond. Soon, a big gray wolf trotted across the hillside, mountains rising behind it, Slough Creek flowing in the valley below.

"It's Odin," Toni said quietly.

Trotting just behind him was a black wolf with a white triangle and a two-toned wolf. The black and two-toned wolves turned and headed down to an aspen grove near Slough Creek, but the gray wolf didn't follow. The large gray wolf stopped for a short while on the side of the hill, looking out over his domain, his stance filled with confidence and power.

Buck reached over and froze the image.

"We don't need to watch anymore," he said. "Let's remember him like that."

TAKE 28:

"AT THE END OF THE FIRST YEAR OF THE YELLOWSTONE WOLF RESTORATION PROJECT, TWENTY-ONE WOLVES, DIVIDED BETWEEN THREE PACKS, LIVED IN THE PARK. ALTHOUGH THE NUMBERS CHANGE FROM YEAR TO YEAR, THE PARK'S POPULATION IS NOW 108 WOLVES IN ELEVEN PACKS, AND IN THE GREATER YELLOWSTONE ECOSYSTEM MORE THAN 500 WOLVES."

MONDAY, MAY 19

The next morning, the sun was just peeking over the mountains when everyone piled into Isabel's SUV. Buck sat up front between Isabel and Lobo. Toni sat in the back between Dad and Shoop. Except for a few comments about the landscape, they were quiet until they drove across the bridge over the Yellowstone River. Then Shoop started humming.

"Shoop!" Toni exclaimed. "Stop! That's what Lyall whistled."

A sheepish grin spread across Shoop's face. "Sorry," he said. "Ever since you told me about that, the tune has been in my head. I was just looking out the window and didn't even realize I was humming it."

"It seems familiar to me, too," Lobo said, "but I can't place it."

"It's from *Peter and the Wolf*," Toni said.

"You said that yesterday to Lyall," Buck said. "I've never heard of it."

"It's a fairy tale and symphony combined," Toni said. "A narrator tells the story, but the different instruments in the orchestra are the characters. My first-grade music teacher used it to teach us the sounds of different instruments."

"And Toni loved it so much, she begged for the CD for her birthday," Shoop added. "We had to hear it over and over and over."

"What's it about?" Buck asked.

"Peter is a young boy who decides to go wolf hunting with his popgun, and he ends up capturing the wolf by the tail using a rope. Peter's character is played by a string quartet; the wolf, by the horns."

"And a flute is a bird," Shoop added, "but the grandpa was my favorite—he was a bassoon."

Everyone chuckled, and then Lobo spoke up.

"There are a lot of stories where the wolf is the bad character," he said. "Many were made up as warnings to kids to be careful—there are bad things out in the world."

"Yeah, you two kids should have paid more attention to those fairy tales," Dad said. The night before, when they got back to their campsite, both Buck and Toni had been reprimanded about their decision to hide in Lyall's truck. Now Buck was worried Dad was starting up again in front of Isabel and Lobo.

"But the fairy tales always have heroes," Buck said, and when Dad reached over the seat and tousled Buck's hair, the boy let out a sigh of relief.

"I know, son," Dad said. "And I'm proud of you and Toni. You were the heroes in this case."

Isabel slowed down and turned onto Slough Creek Road but immediately stopped. A sawhorse barricade with a sign saying ROAD CLOSED sat in the middle of the drive. Lobo and Buck got out of the SUV. They each took one end of the sawhorse and put it in the back of the vehicle. They got back inside, and soon the SUV pulled up alongside the road where the spotters had been parked three days before. Everyone climbed out, and Buck put his binoculars to his eyes. Isabel opened the back of the vehicle. Toni grabbed Isabel's binoculars as Lobo took out his and Isabel's spotting scope cases. Then Shoop reached in for his camera case.

With the binoculars, Buck found the dead tree trunk, moved his eyes up the hillside and a little to the left of the bleached-white bison skull, and then on up to the dark hole with the flattened dirt area in front.

"Freki's out on the patio," Buck said. "And there are two pups out there—the black one and the two-toned."

"Geri's over to the side," Toni added. "She just came out of the junipers and lay down in the sun."

Soon, the spotting scopes were set up, and as Shoop filmed, the others took turns with the scopes and the binoculars. Jord came out of the den, the gray pup following her. The black alpha female walked over to Geri, sniffed at her, and then lay down beside her two-toned pack mate. The pups played, rolling over each other, nipping at each other's ears, and climbing over Freki.

"Look!" Buck suddenly exclaimed, now looking through Lobo's spotting scope. "There's another two-toned wolf. It's coming out of the junipers where Geri had been."

"Let me take a quick look," Lobo said. Buck stepped aside, taking the binoculars Lobo handed him. "That's 847M—a male that left Mollie's pack two years ago and has been a loner. I haven't seen him for a while, but I recognize him by his very dark ears."

"Mollie's pack?" Buck asked.

"It's another pack south of here," Isabel answered. "Mollie's pack is the biggest pack currently in the park, with eighteen wolves this year."

"Has he come in to take Odin's place?" Toni asked, looking through Isabel's spotting scope. She stepped aside and let Dad take a look.

"Yes, most likely," Lobo said.

"He's gone over to lay next to Geri and Jord," Buck stated.

"I guess they have accepted him into the pack," Lobo said.

They continued to watch the wolves for another twenty minutes. All the while Jord, Geri, and 847M lay in the sun. Suddenly Jord jumped up. She trotted over to Freki, who also stood up, and soon Geri and 847M came over to the den as well.

"What's going on?" Buck said.

"Maybe they're going hunting," Toni said.

"I don't know," Lobo said. "Keep watching."

The adult wolves stood near the den for a couple of minutes, the young playing in front. Then Jord started trotting off toward the top of the hill behind the den, 847M right behind her. Geri and Freki both looked up toward them. Next Freki nudged the black pup with her nose and, turning to the gray pup, nudged it as well. The two pups stopped playing and headed toward the den entrance, but Geri pushed them aside. Freki now nudged the two-toned pup and then trotted around it, heading up the hill. All three pups started following her, with Geri in the rear, occasionally pushing the pups along. Jord and

847M had reached the top of the hill and stood, looking back down toward the den. They waited until Freki, Geri, and the three pups reached them. Then turning, the whole pack disappeared over the hill.

"That's the last we'll see of them for a while," Lobo said, taking the binoculars from his eyes. "They're going to their rendezvous site."

"One big, happy family," Toni stated.

"Yes," Buck agreed. "Running wild, where they should be."

GLOSSARY

ALPHA WOLVES: The breeding pair of a wolf pack. Also used to describe the dominant male and female leaders.

ASPERGER'S SYNDROME: A mild form of autism that is characterized by difficulty with social interaction. People with Asperger's may avoid making eye contact or may interpret language in a literal manner (based on exactly how something is said, not an intended meaning). People with Asperger's usually have normal to high intelligence and may be extremely interested in and knowledgeable about a specific topic.

BIODIVERSITY: The variety of all living things. An area with a high amount of biodiversity has many different kinds of living animals and plants dwelling there.

BISON: American bison, inaccurately called buffalo, is the largest land mammal in North America and the national mammal of the United States. Males are called bulls; females, cows; and young are called calves.

BOILING POINT: The temperature at which a liquid begins to boil. At sea level, the boiling point of water is 212 degrees Fahrenheit, but boiling point temperatures decrease (become less) as elevations, or height of the land, increase (become higher).

CHANNEL: A path cut through rock or dirt by water.

DEADFALL: Dead trees that have fallen to the ground.

DRONE: An unmanned aircraft flown by remote control.

ECOSYSTEM: A community of all the animals and plants that depend on and interact with one another in a specific environment or area.

ELK: One of the largest members of the Cervidae family, which also includes deer, moose, and caribou. Males, called bulls, weigh up to 730 pounds, are almost five feet tall at the shoulder, and have large antlers that they shed each year. Females are called cows and do not grow antlers. Young elk are called calves.

FAMILY: The scientific classification of animals and plants that all have similar characteristics. For example, moose, elk, caribou, and deer are all in the same family.

FIELD OF VISION: Described in degrees of a circle (a circle is 360 degrees), the field of vision is the entire area that can be seen when staring straight ahead, including what's in front and to the sides.

FRACTURE: A crack in Earth's crust (or top layer) caused by weather, pressure, or movement, such as earthquakes. Fractures can be as small as a hair or as large as a continent.

FUMAROLE (pronounced FYOO-ma-roll): A fracture, or crack in the earth, that releases steam and gases with temperatures of up to 750 degrees Fahrenheit. Also called vents.

GEOTHERMAL: Related to the internal heat of Earth. (Geo means "Earth," thermal means "heat.") Geysers, hot springs, fumaroles, and mud pots are types of geothermal features.

GEYSER (pronounced GI-zer): A hot spring that period-ically erupts, shooting extremely hot water and steam into the air.

HABITUATED: Becoming used to something, such as a wild animal becoming used to being around people.

HOT SPRING: Naturally heated underground water that flows to Earth's surface.

LODGEPOLE PINE: A tall, slender variety of pine that grows in northwestern North America, named for its long, straight trunk that was frequently used by Native Americans to build lodges.

MAGPIE: Common in the western half of North America, the black-billed magpie is a member of the Corvidae family, which includes crows, ravens, and jays. A magpie has a twenty-four-inch wingspan, and its twelve-inch tail is as long as its body. It is black with white shoulders and belly and iridescent dark blue-green wings and tail.

METRICS: A system of measurement based on tens. Length is measured in millimeters (mm), centimeters (cm), meters (m), and kilometers (km). Weight is measured in grams (gm) and kilograms (kg).

MICROORGANISM: A living thing that can be seen only by using a microscope. These include bacteria, some kinds of fungi and algae, and other types of organisms.

MINERAL: Solid nonliving substances that were formed in the earth by nature. Some minerals, such as sulfur, are nonmetallic. Others, such as iron, are metallic.

MUD POT: A kind of hot spring in which steam and gases bubble up explosively through muddy clay, forming mud bubbles that spurt and splatter with gurgling noises, and sometimes shoot mud up to fifteen feet into the air. Artists' Paintpots is the name of an area of mud pots in Yellowstone.

PHYSICS: The science of matter (things that have mass and take up space) and its motion and how it interacts with energy and force. Physics includes the study of light, heat, sound, electricity, and mechanics.

QUADCOPTER: An aircraft with four rotors, or spinning blades, that are used to lift and propel it.

RAVEN: Abundant in western and northeastern North America, the common raven is a member of the Corvidae family, which includes crows, magpies, and jays. Ravens are entirely black with a large, thick beak and a forty-eight-inch wingspan.

RENDEZVOUS SITE (pronounced RON-day-voo): An area a wolf pack uses as its "home base" after the denning period and prior to nomadic hunting period. A single wolf pack may have up to six different rendezvous sites.

RIVULET: A little stream of water.

SPECIES: A scientific categorization of animals or plants that are able to reproduce with one another, producing offspring of the same species.

SULFUR: A yellow chemical element. Pure sulfur has no smell, but when combined with gases, it produces odors. Hydrogen sulfide, an extremely poisonous gas that contains sulfur and smells like rotten eggs, is often released from geysers and fumaroles.

SUPERVOLCANO: A supervolcano has a thousand times more magma, or molten rock, than a regular volcano, and has a caldera (a large, bowl-shaped crater) instead of a volcanic cone. The Yellowstone caldera is thirty-five miles wide and forty-five miles long.

THERMOPHILE: A bacteria or other living microorganism that lives in habitats with extremely high temperatures.

VELVET: A soft, hairy layer of skin covering a new and growing antler. Velvet provides oxygen and nutrients to the developing bone.

WAPITI (pronounced WAH-pit-tee): The Native American Shawnee tribe's word for elk.

JUDY YOUNG

Judy Young is the award-winning author of more than two dozen children's books, including the first two books in The Wild World of Buck Bray series, *The Missing Grizzly Cubs* and *Danger at the Dinosaur Stomping Grounds*. Her books also include the middle-grade novel *Promise* and several historical fiction picture books. Judy resides with her husband, Ross, in the mountains of Mink Creek, Idaho, and is only a few hours from Yellowstone National Park, where she frequently camps, fishes, hikes, rides horses, watches out for grizzlies, and goes wolf spotting. For a behind-the-scenes adventure in the wild world of Buck Bray, visit "Buck Bray Scrapbook" on Judy's website at www.judyyoungpoetry.com.

OTHER BOOKS _IN_ THIS SERIES

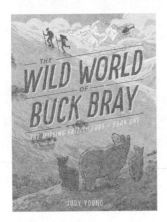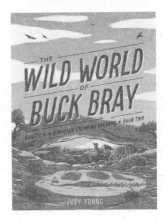

The Wild World of Buck Bray: *The Missing Grizzly Cubs*

As the star of a new kid-oriented wilderness show, eleven-year-old Buck Bray travels to Denali National Park to shoot the first episode. Buck's annoyed when the cameraman's daughter, Toni, unexpectedly shows up. But the kids band together when they realize two grizzly cubs are missing, and they work to solve the mystery.

The Wild World of Buck Bray: *Danger at the Dinosaur Stomping Grounds*

In the sequel to *The Missing Grizzly Cubs*, Buck and Toni and the Buck Bray TV crew head to Utah's Canyonlands National Park to film an episode. There Buck and Toni find themselves in danger at the Dinosaur Stomping Grounds, as they try to discover who is behind the vandalization and theft of the area's ancient artifacts.

Enjoy Another Middle-Grade Offering by
Judy Young
PROMISE

"The town of Promise is a tight-knit one, but 11-year-old Kaden has always been on the outside, with only a half-tame raven for a friend. He and his strict grandmother live simply just outside the town limits and keep to themselves, barely acknowledging their old family shame: Kaden's father has been in jail for theft most of the boy's life. When he is released from prison and returns to Promise, Kaden's father turns his son's life upside down. . . . A bold look at the little-discussed subject of the prison system and the stigma that surrounds the families of the incarcerated."— *Booklist*